W9-BII-763

Frostbite

Eric Pete

www.urbanbooks.net

Urban Books, LLC
78 East Industry Court
Deer Park, NY 11729

ISBN 13: 978-1-60162-337-9
ISBN 10: 1-60162-337-2

First Trade Paperback Printing March 2012
Printed in the United States of America

10 9 8 7 6 5 4 3 2 1

This is a work of fiction. Any references or similarities to actual events, real people, living, or dead, or to real locales are intended to give the novel a sense of reality. Any similarity in other names, characters, places, and incidents is entirely coincidental.

Distributed by Kensington Publishing Corp.
Submit Wholesale Orders to:
Kensington Publishing Corp.
C/O Penguin Group (USA) Inc.
Attention: Order Processing
405 Murray Hill Parkway
East Rutherford, NJ 07073-2316
Phone: 1-800-526-0275
Fax: 1-800-227-9604

Acknowledgments

Welcome to the further adventures of Truth North, a creation who takes my love of flawed characters to another level. Based on the readers' reaction and the fun I had with *Crushed Ice,* I saw there was still more trouble I could cook up for him. *Especially if Sophia's anywhere in the picture*. But with this one, I wanted to see how Truth handled trouble not of his making and way out of his comfort zone. So, here we are with *Frostbite*. I hope you enjoy.

I also want to thank you for spending not just your hard-earned money, but for spending your precious time with me. I sincerely hope that you continue to come back because there are many more stories to tell and journeys to take.

To my family, friends, agent, publisher, and fellow authors; thank you for being there. This year has been a challenge, but I wouldn't trade it for anything and am a better person for it.

One love, one heart.

Can't stop. Won't stop. Believe that.

-Eric

@IAmEricPete

NOW

"Please. Please. I don't want to die!" she screams. Pitch perfect.

"So . . . what's it going to be?" I say to the man who just listened to the woman's pleas. It's his wife. He knows it now.

"Now look here . . ."

"Don't stall. You'll only make it worse for her. And your kid."

"I'll kill you! I swear to God, I will—"

"Do what I say. You will do what I say," I utter, completing his statement for him.

I check my watch while he comes to grips with his new reality.

"Okay. Okay. How can I trust you?" he asks, stifling a stutter that I still notice.

"You can't," I say calmly. "No one can trust me."

1

Last Year
Florida . . . Somewhere

No one was home when my phone rang, vibrating just once in my pocket. They were all away at the movies. Saw when they pulled away in the Range Rover. Even the maid had the night off. Probably out celebrating their son's status as the consensus number one recruit in the country. Kid played football for St. Thomas Aquinas over in Fort Lauderdale.

The dad was an investment banker. Successful even by the standards of the old economy—the bullshit, happy-happy fantasy we believed in before the bottom fell out. Maybe it was because of people like him that things were in such a shitty state. I mean . . . I know I took a hit with my nest egg. My client could've been one of the people he'd fucked over.

But that wasn't the reason I was hired.

It was simple petty jealousy.

Y'see . . . my client had a son as well.

The kids were goddamn teammates even.

Except my client's kid was the consensus number two recruit in the country.

But like the wise poet Nelly once said, "Two is not a winner and three nobody remembers."

Competition on steroids.

A simple planting of evidence and the dad would be besieged by legal problems with ethics violations. Legal problems that would be a distraction for his entire family as well as his son.

Distraction enough to underperform in the upcoming all-star games in which they were scheduled to participate. And providing the case why numero *dos* should be numero *uno*. Wasn't like both didn't have a crazy share of scholarship offers anyway.

And if I didn't take the job, my client was going to have someone else pull a Tonya Harding and break the kid's leg. Or worse if they were amateurs. At least this way, no one was physically hurt.

Sick shit, but I just took the money.

"Hello?" I whispered as I swiftly removed the flash drive from the home office computer I'd hacked into. Had to be sure to reset the security system on my way out.

"Mr. Elvis? Elvis Spielberg?" the woman asked upon my answering, almost daring to laugh at the implausible name. Most people chuckled when they heard it. Didn't care. Wasn't my real name anyway. Just another guise that suited my needs like the set of clothes I wore.

But almost no one who knew me by that name would have this phone number.

Almost no one.

That's what really piqued my curiosity.

"Yes. This is he. Who is this?" I asked, as I backtracked, making sure everything in the home was left undisturbed. The ID said UNKNOWN CALLER.

She didn't identify herself. "I'm calling for Aswad," she offered instead.

"Who?" I asked as I checked my watch. Was on a short schedule. "I don't know any 'Aswad.'"

"I'm sorry. That is what he calls her. She said to tell you her name is Sophia." A mix of fondness and irritation gripped me. We weren't on the best of terms when we parted ways. A difference of opinion about my vision or something. In short, she was greedy and reckless. Probably the reason I was getting this call. After originally being part of a plot against me, the woman was now part protégé/part problem with me never being too clear on which.

"And where is Sophia for you to be calling on her behalf?" I asked, trying to place the woman's accent and gauge whether she was lying. The home's security system central keypad was in front of me. Another minute and this job would be completed except for my money.

Money from my client who was also this guy's neighbor.

No cup of sugar. Just a dose of scorpion venom served up.

Like I said, *competition on steroids.*

"Miami," the woman on the phone replied. Some sick coincidence that I was already in south Florida? Or was Sophia up to her usual tricks?

"Bullshit," I hissed. "She's in London." Remembered feeling the inside of her hand aboard the Eye while staring out over the Thames. We were playing tourists . . . and lovers that day. Some welcome downtime while traipsing across Europe. And a fitting reward after getting my revenge on.

"No, sir. She is in America. I . . . I just saw her. This morning when I was cleaning. She said she needs you to come quick."

"Okay," I mumbled as I wiped the codes showing my entrance and soon-to-be exit from the security system memory and took my leave. "And what else?"

"And that you'd reward me for delivering this message."

Greed.

Now that was real.

Guess I was starting to believe this woman who'd called me.

"What's your price?" I asked as I slipped into the darkness where I felt most comfortable.

2

After agreeing to get her family into the country from the Philippines, the cleaning lady who called for Sophia provided me with the details I needed. Then I had to offer up another ten thousand to get some rather unique information from her.

In the end, the conclusion was the same.

Sophia was in a world of shit.

So with short notice and scant recon, I'd come to Coral Gables preparing to do something foolish. Things like this usually took twice as long for which to prepare. Can't say I didn't like a challenge, but lives could be on the line if I miscalculated this. Including mine.

The sun beamed through the front window of the van as I checked my watch and adjusted my uniform.

"Your country appreciates your cooperation," I recited all official like a final time before the three of us exited the repair van.

"Yeah, yeah. No problem. We got it. Anything to help bring down terrorists," the burly *Cubano* in the driver's seat grunted. It was as if his hardhat were two sizes too small for his head.

"Sir, I never said these gentlemen were terrorists. This is only an intelligence gathering mission," I corrected him. "And we're trusting you to keep quiet about anything you witness today. But if your bosses give you any grief, just call the number for the State Department on the card I gave you." In case one of them had called the dummy number with the DC area code already, I'd left a prerecorded message that sounded authentic and mysterious.

"Probably goin' plant some bugs like on *Mission Impossible,* ain't ya? Shit, bosses should give us both promotions. Or maybe new black Dodges," the tall, lanky Haitian kid who was the apprentice joked. I'd been listening to him brag for the last half hour about his test scores in electronics school. And about that same black Dodge Charger he wanted so badly.

Hated going this route. One thing I never did was pose as a Fed. To do so was to paint a shiny red bull's-eye on one's self. There was no time to do this all nice and tidy. I was just lucky my idea of an official badge and ID fooled my newly drafted coworkers. I preferred working through intermediaries like them, but was putting myself directly in harm's way for Sophia.

Sophia.

A unique relationship in my unusual life I had with her.

But I had to focus on what was before me.

Not the past we may or may not have had.

"Let's go. I'm sure they're waiting on us," I said as I slammed the door on the imprisoned memory of Jason North once again and slid open the door to the van to the light of day.

The three of us—the driver, Alonzo, the kid, Jeff, and I—grabbed our equipment and went on our call for a rush repair order on a satellite TV outage.

Today had to be the day.

That's why I shut down their satellite feed last night while everyone slept.

Just off Old Dixie Highway and near the University

of Miami, we buzzed the front door to the unassuming ceramic-roofed compound shrouded in palm trees. The plaque on the front of the secure facility and the colorful flag flying overhead identified the place as a consulate for one of those tiny Middle Eastern nations. The ones with more money than they have people. And where they import staff from third-world countries to service their needs, no matter how basic or base they might be.

After buzzing in and posing for the camera, the three of us were met by two suited men who looked like they were sumo wrestlers crammed into Hugo Boss tablecloths. They proceeded to inspect our identification badges with intense scrutiny then crosschecked the names against the approved list. After that, we were frisked and patted down. Lucky for me, they were only feeling for something that could be a weapon.

"What took you so long?" one of them asked, chastising us. "The prince is about to throw a fit."

"Traffic," Alonzo offered with a shrug. "Is the outage affecting all the TVs?"

"Of course. We almost left for the yacht to catch the Cup, but there are too many people to relocate on such short notice, so hurry up. Please."

"It will be faster if the three of us split up," Alonzo commented. "Someone needs to inspect the junction box and satellite's dish arrays while the rest check the lines and individual receivers. How many TVs do you have in here anyway?"

Our greeter laughed. "More than you can imagine. Go ahead and split up," he agreed while checking his watch. "But keep your badges displayed. I'll go check on the prince and give him an update. Important friends of his are here and they're already placing bets on the game. Going to miss the first pitch. Hopefully, he doesn't have me beheaded." From his expression, one couldn't tell if he was joking about the beheading thing, but . . .

"I'll check the individual units," I volunteered lazily as we'd already agreed. "Where should I start?"

"The large television in the viewing room where the prince is at," he replied. "The sooner you can get that one working, the better for all of us."

"Probably should start with the smaller ones. These are all wired in a series of F switches before they transitioned to the standard safeguards and redundancies. The culprit is usually with the TVs that don't get much attention," I said, making up some gibberish and waving my arms like I was a pro. Last thing I wanted was to go anywhere near a crowd.

"Uh . . . okay," he replied. "Well, start with the unoccupied rooms. But stay away from the private quarters or any room that is locked," he said, trying to size me up. I acted as if one of my eyes was slightly crossed, disturbing him to no end.

I saw the cleaning lady who'd called me the other night. She wore orange to identify herself today. As she walked by the three of us, I began humming an Elvis tune, "Heartbreak Hotel," for her to identify me. In the open-air center of the compound was a large swimming pool with intricate, mosaic tile patterns, which she navigated past. As I moved steadily along with my clipboard, I saw her stop by a locked door on the second floor balcony where she paused to draw an imaginary "X" across its exterior. Just as she did that, I could hear a cacophony of loud voices shouting in Arabic that echoed off the walls. Probably beginning to complain about our keeping them from the UAFA Arab Nations Cup they were assembled to watch today.

Prince Abdel Al-Bin Sada was a big fan of the world's version of football. After a massive fight at one of the venues in Dubai last year, he'd been kindly asked through intermediaries in his royal family, in the most polite way possible, to stay away for the next half decade. According to my research, the storied prince's passion for his country's national pastime was equally met by his passion for the flesh of women other than his wife.

Seeing the time displayed on my watch, I needed to speed up my inspection and troubleshooting ruse. With rough schematics of the place, I'd told my two role players where to be when service was restored. Coming to the door marked with the magic "X," I took another glance to make sure no one was nearby. With the security cameras and armed detail inside, they'd become complacent here in this south Florida community of old money.

At the designated time, I began counting down.

Then, just as the satellite service was restored, all gathered downstairs on the opposite side of the compound broke out in raucous cheers and jubilation. And at that moment as the game was on, it *really was on*. Disguised by the festive noises, I put my shoulder into the door and partially busted it open. Grimacing from the pain and scared of there being an alarm, I backed up and swiftly kicked the door where it had been weakened.

It did have an alarm.

Shrill and piercing, I tried to block it out as I entered to see seven scared women, all of them beautiful, exotic, and scantily clad, huddled together on the oversized bed.

A modern-day harem for the prince's pleasure.

And there was *Aswad* in the middle.

Aswad. Arabic for black.

Real creative, that prince.

Adrenaline took over. "Hurry! If you want to get out of here, go straight to the back. There's a boat waiting on the waterway."

But they were stunned into inactivity. None wanting to be the first to make a move. Or listen to a total stranger posing as a satellite repairman.

"Go! Now! Freedom!" I shouted, this time in shoddy Arabic, to light a fire under them.

Four of them scurried out, briefly making eye contact to thank me, while two remained resolute atop the bed, glaring at me in disgust. Different strokes for different folks I suppose.

Sophia ran into my arms and held me. "Truth," was all she said. Faintly. Softly. The flowing minimal fabric seemed to almost hover on her body and she smelled of exotic oils. My past sexual partner—and once protégé—awakened disparate emotions that I quickly shoved aside.

"C'mon," I said as I dropped my hardhat and rapidly led Sophia by the arm. We bounded down the stairs, almost three at a time, until reaching the ground floor and facing the large pool.

"I thought you were in London," I offered as I yanked her along.

"I was," Sophia replied. "That's where I met the prince."

"Uh huh," I said, neither approving nor condemning her choices.

"Hey!" my original greeter yelled almost directly across the pool from us. He'd emerged in response to the alarm and wasn't alone. Three more slabs of meat in suits, probably representing a veritable United Nations, fanned out in a protective pattern from behind him, all going for whatever firearms they carried. At that point, I dumped the remainder of my worker gear and broke into a full-on sprint.

As she struggled to stay on her feet, Sophia protested in my ear. “Why aren’t we taking the waterway out back like you said? You’re going to get us killed!” she screamed.

But there was no escape out back. That was all a diversion that was just now coming into play as the four other kept women were spotted scattering all over the compound in a panic. With some of his people distracted by their sudden appearance, the head of security hollered at us again.

“Stop!” he barked as I could now see the front door in sight.

“You don’t know these people. He’s going to kill us! He’s going to kill us!” Sophia cried as I felt her nails dig into my hand. Her fear was genuine.

“Shut up and strip!” I yelled to her as I took the barest of glimpses at my watch.

“Huh? Are you fuckin’ crazy?”

“Strip. Do it now!” I commanded with an angered, desperate look on my face that told her not to question me. I didn’t like being called crazy.

With each awkward, quickened step, we both began discarding articles of clothing in our wake. Sophia must’ve thought this was some attempt to trip our pursuer up like in the cartoons. If only my gamble were less desperate than that.

With the electronically locked front doors to the compound mere feet away, a bullet rang out just missing my face. It ricocheted off the reinforced metal making both of us skittishly hop in surprise. They figured we were cornered, but probably didn't want to chance us getting any closer to the street outside . . . and American soil.

With the two of us buck naked and back into a full-on sprint, I pushed the button on the only other piece of electronics I had remaining in my possession besides my watch. Praying it was the right frequency, I heard the front doors click with recognition. Had scanned for the proper code when we arrived.

Despite his size, the prince's head of security was closing on us. And no way in hell did I think he'd politely stop at the door's edge and let us get away. And with just my birthday suit and Sophia in tow, I wasn't equipped to wage an unarmed war with a pro.

The hot, humid smell of freedom greeted our noses as Sophia and I rushed out the front and bolted onto the sidewalk.

"What the fuck?" Sophia gasped at the sight that awaited her.

Dozens upon dozens of people stood before us in carefully formed lines in the middle of South Alhambra Circle, others still joining them. Like troops awaiting their general's instructions.

Men and women.

Mostly brown in skin tone like us, but comprised of all different races and ethnicities with dashes of vanilla thrown in among them.

All matching approximately our heights and builds.

And all nude.

Right as we stepped into the mass of bodies, they began the choreographed routine to Flo Rida's "Club Can't Handle Me" that blared from the speakers positioned on the flatbed truck stopped behind them.

The prince's security emerged onto the sidewalk with guns drawn, but were stunned by what they were witnessing.

"Quick. Follow along and do what everybody else is doing," I hissed in her ear as we gradually moved to the rear of the hastily assembled flash mob. I'd arranged for them on one of the online social networking sites last night, providing instructions on the time and routine along with a phony cause célèbre for which to bare all.

The riskiest part of this plan and they'd actually come through.

With us blending in and the prince's not wanting an international incident, they holstered their firearms then slowly retreated inside the compound to finish rounding up the other captive women . . . and questioning the real satellite repair workers. But not before a couple of them smiled at the nude bodies bouncing and gyrating in front of them.

Exhausted and drained, I backed away from the still performing flash mob and bent over, succumbing to the adrenaline fleeing my body as I took a minute to catch my breath.

"Well . . . you look good," Sophia commented as she smacked me on my bare ass, bopping around as if the terror and drama of the last few minutes hadn't even happened. And ignoring that she was standing nude in Coral Gables.

But she could get away with being nude as beautiful as she was.

"Who are all these people?"

"Students. From the U," I said, managing to point in the general direction of the university campus on the other side of Old Dixie Highway. "I needed young, willing bodies from nearby."

"Never knew you were a Canes fan," she somehow joked.

"I'm not. Florida State fan," I replied, still trying to get my heart rate under control and gasping for air. "But I'd never put their students in harm's way," I joked back. "Now let's get to the clothes I stashed before the cops show up."

Fully clothed again, I turned up the CNN broadcast with Soledad O'Brien. Another one of those specials they gave her carte blanche to host. *Black In America XII: The Blackest Ever* or something like that.

We were near the edge of the Everglades. At the Crowne Plaza by Sawgrass Mills in Sunrise. Two queen-sized beds at my request. Sophia was in the bathroom using the rinse for her hair that I'd bought along with a few sets of clothes and luggage from the mall across the street.

My plan was to lay low and fly out of Fort Lauderdale Airport tonight. If the prince was as manic about his possessions as he was about his soccer matches then unlimited wealth could be troublesome even for a plotter and schemer like me.

"How do I look, baby?" Sophia asked as she emerged from the bathroom, hair damp and body rolled into a hotel towel. Her hair was back to black now. A change from the honey blond worn by her to please the little prince no doubt. Then she dropped the towel for dramatic effect, never one for modesty. Body was still as I remembered it. Bangin'. Pussy probably as good as always.

That not-so-secret weapon of hers.

But under me she'd gained other weapons for her arsenal.

Under me.

Seeing that look in her eyes, hearing that sexy little sucking sound she makes through her teeth when she cums.

Hard not to go there considering our history.

"Need me to tell you?" I replied, taking my own path. A question for a question as I stepped aside and went toward the bathroom. Pretending to be unfazed by her.

"No. But a girl can never get too much reassurance," Sophia said as I gazed at her reflection in the mirror. Saw her wink.

"I'm glad . . . you're okay," I offered. I really was glad she was okay. Once upon a time I wanted to kill her myself. Almost did. But that was another time. When we were on different sides in a game in which I was unaware I was a participant.

"Don't see you expressing your relief."

"I got you out, right? Should be enough," I shot back, knowing how Sophia *expressed* herself. She was kinda like a guy in terms of sex. Sometimes she just wanted it. Other times it was to serve as a distraction or relieve stress. And probably nothing more stressful than being someone's captive for who knows how long. But sex also could be a way of apologizing.

Yet Sophia never apologized for anything.

Couldn't start thinking that way about her.

That she was suddenly caring and considerate.

And worthy of me reciprocating.

Thinking like that cost me before.

Almost my life.

"Fuck it. Want to play the game? Fine," she spat as she stormed over to the shopping bags gathered atop her bed. "And where have you been anyway? That wasn't the first time I'd tried getting a message out to you."

"On jobs," I replied. "Thought I wasn't needed anyway. And what kind of luck do you have? A fucking harem?"

"Long story," she replied, avoiding the topic yet again. I could somewhat fill in the blanks, but wanted her to come clean.

A lesson for both of us.

"What happened back in London after I left you?" I inquired.

"You mean after I left *you?*" Sophia corrected me. My mouth clenched, but I quickly relented. Had taught her too much about reading micro expressions, the tiny facial tics that most people were unaware they had. But that told a whole world of information.

"Let's agree that we had our differences," I said.

"Sure did. You wanted to skulk around in the shadows. Like a fuckin' Phantom of the Opera," she ridiculed.

"And you wanted to be the center of attention. All bright and shiny like the sun. A big ball of hot gas," I shot back. "Not like I taught you. See where it got you."

"A lot of money. Pounds, euros, lira, dollars. That's where it got me," she mused while removing the clothes from the bags and holding them up for inspection. I wished that she would hurry and put something on.

But she didn't.

Just kept switching her weight from leg to leg in a rhythmic case of nerves.

"Come clean. What did you do?" I asked.

"Nothing," she said as she held up a blouse that obscured her breasts for the barest of moments. Then she turned her back to me to dig through more clothes.

"Bullshit," I said as I admired her silhouette.

"Okay," she said with a false sigh, having strung me along enough to her satisfaction. "The prince's wife. She was worried he was getting too serious with one of his many women. I was supposed get inside and do some digging. Play around. Figure out which one and let her take care of the rest. Involuntary severance."

"And?"

"Motherfucker became too sweet on me for her. Bitch had a change of heart. Broke our agreement then snitched me out. Of course, he didn't kill me. This shit too good for that," she said with a cocky smile as she tapped a fingertip near her clit. "Instead, the fucker threw me in with the rest of 'em bitches and I been on lockdown since."

"I'm sorry."

"Hey. Ain't your fault. The opulence suited me, but I ain't nobody's slave. That was some crazy shit you pulled back there to get me out."

"Are you thanking me?" I asked.

"What if I am?"

We shared a glance as she prepared for my next move. I thought it over rather than succumbing to her blatant charms. Got ready to take a nice cold shower instead. Get my head right . . . both of them. "Flight outta here leaves in about four hours. I hope those clothes fit . . . and that your size hasn't changed," I joked as I prepared for her complaints over designer label versus store brand.

"I just hope there's a swimsuit in here."

"Huh?" I blurted, sticking my head from out of the bathroom.

"Oh I'm not ready to leave yet," Sophia said, an innocent look used as a disguise.

3

"We should go," I said as I surveyed the surroundings, never one to let down my guard. Not even in these kinds of surroundings.

"You don't tell me what to do!" Sophia snapped. Inglewood was strong in every syllable as she voiced her frustration with my playing the mother hen.

But instead of being in Cali or anywhere else for that matter, we were still in Florida.

South Beach to be exact.

Poolside VIP at the W.

Sophia swatted away my hand as I reached to stop her again. Felt like old times.

The bad old times.

When, beyond the sex and chaos, we realized not much else could be there.

For I was a non-person absent a heart.

Afrojack had just finished a set this evening. Now Taio Cruz was taking the poolside stage with throngs of bikini-clad senoritas shaking and popping their asses in the cool, refreshing breeze coming off the beach below.

"Best that we go," I said again as the bass assaulted our ears and the intoxicated crowd roared.

"After my captivity? I just want to live a little! Can a sista do that? Huh? Can a sista just live?" she hollered a little too loud for my liking, already a few too many drinks in her, before joining the other women dancing to the music.

"Which is exactly why we need to go," I mumbled to no one but myself as I stood there, one of the few people not in high spirits this evening. I didn't feel comfortable staying around Miami a minute longer, that danger clock steadily ticking—especially after back-to-back jobs—but couldn't blame her for wanting to cut loose.

Besides, maybe I was being too paranoid—nerves worn from years of schemes and lies leaving me a wounded veteran. More so, it was of what Sophia reminded me. A time when I'd fooled myself into believing a fairy tale of my own creation. And wound up being caught with my guard down.

My mind flashed back to the New Mexico desert. Hot sand beneath my broken feet once again. Bullets and blood. Sweaty, out of breath, and my life hanging in the balance. The man learned to be a jackrabbit that day.

But Sophia could have her fun . . . for a little while longer. I just needed to stay busy and not dwell on such things. As I brought up a secure link on my cell, I signaled to the still-dancing Sophia that I had to take a call then left poolside. She was relatively safe and in public view, so her dismissive nod was acceptable.

Down in the lobby of the W, full of free Wi-Fi signals and everything else coming at a price, I opened a communications line long unused.

U still out there? I typed, feeling a little foolish.

U alive? came a response after a long pause. Part of me wished no reply had come. While another part welcomed the once customary banter that I shared with Lorelei Smart, the young woman on the other end of the exchange.

Appears that way, huh? I typed back.

Yeah. It's you. Cocky mofo still. No one else knows to reach me this way. Been years. What up?

Relax. Just saying hi.

Hi then. No dirt to sell? You were the best. I miss those days.

Even the way it ended?

W/ u showing up at my job and threatening me? Yeah. No worries. U were under a lot of pressure. People gunnin 4 u. & I didn't help matters.

True. But I spared u. Anyway. Things good?

Yeah. Website goin strong. Peeps gettin the goods 4 me. Not like u, but . . .

There was a pause where I thought we'd been disconnected. Or that she was busy . . . distracted with something more pressing than a man of the shadows who was no longer so invaluable. Then she continued. No longer @ FedEx. U really helped put 4Shizzle on the map w/ ur product, she typed, referring to her Internet gossip site that rivaled TMZ and Media TakeOut these days. Of course, it was nothing to sneeze at back when I would share some of my dirt for side change. But then I found myself her subject rather than source. All of us pawns in a plan to eliminate me because of what I'd discovered about a famous rapper and his sexual preferences.

Ur welcome, I replied.

Where u at these days?

Can't say. U know that, I typed as I came upon a wedding party gathering outside one of the ballrooms. Wealthy Cubans mingling with a smaller family that looked to be Dutch based on their taste in clothes, accents, and body language. Had some brief dealings with them across the pond while Sophia and I were passing through Belgium. They liked to play all leisurely, but were dead serious when it came to business.

I don't know what Lorelei said next for something else suddenly drew all my attention and focus. My turn to be distracted by something more pressing than a gossiping Web blogger no matter how cute and intelligent she was in reality.

Talk l8r, I hastily typed as I switched my phone to a special camera mode. While pretending to view a webcast or something, I angled my phone upward and maneuvered the zoom feature on something dead ahead.

Three rather stoic men had entered the hotel lobby and stopped near the front desk. Rather than staring exposed with my mouth agape, I cautiously backed up, letting the ever-moving wedding party wind around me like a writhing field of human camouflage. The suit I wore was more casual than the male wedding guests', but was sufficient for me to blend in.

"Fuck," I gasped, feeling more stupid than ever for giving in to Sophia.

It was hard not to recognize the largest of the three visitors to the W this evening. The sumo in the finest of tailoring from the prince's compound drew more than just my set of eyes with his imposing girth. New arrivals at the hotel were literally keeping their distance, making the hotel staff curiously nervous. When we'd escaped into the flash mob earlier today, I was more than a little pleased knowing there would be no more run-ins with him.

Ever.

Y'see, I knew his type when I saw 'em.

Man like that was an obsessive professional. Determined to make up for a failure, real or imagined, with no regard for his life. Or the lives of others.

Now, he'd coincidentally shown up here with backup?

As much chance as one of Diddy's artists having success beyond their second album.

I stepped out of the crowd, moving a little closer, confident that I wouldn't be recognized. In the hotel driveway, just outside the revolving door, a long black Audi with diplomatic plates waited. Turning back to the three inside with me, I noticed two of them held something about the size of a cell phone.

Tracking devices.

So, not a coincidence.

Quickly popping into a nearby leather chair, I pretended to check my watch. The large leader gestured for the other two to stay together on the ground floor—presumably to cover any escape—while he followed his signal to the upper levels. As he lumbered up the marble stairs, I was glad to have him away, but knew our reunion would be coming shortly.

If I survived what I planned to do down here.

Oblivious to my being a mere arm's length away, the remaining two walked by, heading toward the wedding party where I'd previously stood. I quickly sprang to my feet, getting a better look over their shoulders at one of the tracking devices. I recognized the model. Made in China. Not the most accurate in this type of environment, but eventually they could find a stationary target.

Even if that target was shaking her ass up at poolside.

With that knowledge, I decided to make my move and eliminate the closest threat. Despite my preference for being hands-off, there was no time. No plot or plan for a situation like this.

Just dive in and get my hands dirty.

"Are you with the bride's or the groom's party?" I asked as I raised the pitch of my voice to an annoying level, circling around and overtaking the two of them. I intentionally entered the space of the one with the tracker. Watched him palm it out of sight as he reacted to me with disgust.

"Get out of my way," he uttered as he surged forward with his mission. He actually assisted me by shielding my hands from his associate. When he tried to blow me off, I struck him with a straight hand directly in the throat. His eyes bulged as he realized his airway was suddenly constricted and my hand in it—pun intended. But he was unable to speak. As he keeled over, I feigned trying to catch him, sure to guide his head into the nearby wall while on the way down. Everyone thought he'd suddenly fainted, which I played to my advantage.

"Somebody get help!" I yelled as I gentled cradled my unconscious victim to the floor. Luckily, I looked far different enough for his associate to not recognize me from my earlier rescue of Sophia.

"Get away from him!" his associate, a no-nonsense type who reeked of blind loyalty, yelled as he gestured me aside. The crowd from the wedding party had gathered round and was overwhelming the conscious one with their incessant chatter. Just as I palmed the tracking device I'd separated from its user and silently withdrew.

Don't know why I bothered looking down at the tracker as I bounded up the stairs. I already knew where I was going with such haste. Just didn't know the hows of Sophia being tracked.

Or why one lone escapee was so important.

Up top, Taio Cruz was thanking everyone for the energy tonight. Probably missed a pretty good show, but

I'd been busy downstairs with one of my own. Didn't take long to spot the mountain moving through the crowd and to quickly shadow him. But he reached the end of his journey all too soon on the edge of the pool. He stood behind an oblivious Sophia, her back turned as his tracking device showed a steady, affixed color. No longer blinking.

Taking a final deep breath, I launched into a brisk jog, bumping other guests as I picked up my pace, rushing headlong into stupidity. I slammed into him from behind, intent on him falling over, but it was like ramming a tree trunk. When he turned around to take a wild swing at whatever irritation had just run into him, I ducked. Before his eyes could fully focus, I sidestepped behind a partygoer only to reemerge at his two o'clock. With a swift, hard sidekick, I drove my foot downward into the side of his knee.

The tree trunk finally budged, grimacing in pain from a buckled knee. When his eyes ignited with recognition of me, I smiled for some hellish reason, further stoking the fires. Something to piss him off and maybe take him off his game. When the mad bull charged, I drove the palm of my hand upward into his nose. Eyes tearing beyond his control, he grabbed at his face, trying to catch my withdrawing hand in the process, but I tugged myself free.

Sophia had finally come back to reality, seeing the spectacle taking place right behind her. I caught a glimpse of the fear etched on her face. Still didn't know how they were tracking her, but we could deal with that later if we made it out alive.

"Run!" I silently mouthed to her. Then like a futile Don Quixote with short-term memory, I rammed the large sumo yet again. Weakened somewhat, his body yielded more than I expected. Or maybe it was his plan, as my momentum drove me into him to where I was unable to regain my balance. Nor pull back.

The two of us plunged into the pool, a big splash resonating on the rooftop as screams rang forth all around us. This time, his grip was unyielding as it clamped onto my sport coat, not allowing me any wiggle room as the other hand took hold of my throat.

As bubbles floated up before my face, I began to panic. Air leaving my lungs, as I now realized he was fast and fluid for his size. And that he could probably swim better than me. I kept trying to kick free, but he was unyielding and weighed me down like an anchor.

Tried to roll once and hoped that we'd separate, but he held on. Even delivering a punch in my eye as I tried to come up for air. I gagged and coughed as we splashed about, considering my options. A knee strike did no good without balance and too much blubber to penetrate. His grip only tightened as his advantage increased. As I felt myself getting lightheaded, I did the only thing left to consider.

I brought my hands up over his face and inserted my thumbs into his eye sockets, pressing as hard as I could.

I imagined what I thought to be a scream. Maybe from him. Maybe from somebody still foolish enough to remain at poolside during our frolic of death.

But like I said. I knew his type.

Even if blinded for life, he wasn't going to let go until I no longer posed a threat.

When I could no longer feel my fingers or tell if they were effective, I knew he'd won. My legs no longer kicked. Body was going in slow motion now as delirium overcame me.

At least Sophia had gotten away.

Knew that girl would be the death . . . of . . . me. . . .

4

Just as the last bits of awareness were leaving me, the water around us sprung to life with new activity. The hotel staff had jumped in, finally doing their job as they swarmed over us in an attempt at breaking up the one-sided scrap. As the big ham-hock loosened his grip in response to the tiny people pulling with all their might, I rolled away from him. Successfully removed my neck from his clutches as I gagged and gasped my way to freedom.

As I struggled to the pool's edge, a familiar hand reached out to me. I crawled up, like some slowed creature washed ashore, coughing and spitting up the water I'd swallowed. Rolling onto my back in exhaustion, I breathed in the air, o sweet air. Sophia bent over me. Held my hand.

"This . . . this is my husband! That man tried to rape me!" she screamed convincingly at the man hotel security was still trying to bring under control. Even in a soaked suit, he was proving elusive. He'd exited the pool too, but on the opposite side. Same position we'd been in earlier today at the compound. But he was determined not to let the two of us slip away this time.

"They're crazy. That man tried to rob me. And she was in on it," he countered calmly. Just enough to cast doubt with the hotel staff who didn't know who to believe. Dripping wet and locking his gaze on the two of us, he breathed evenly. As if I hadn't even given him a decent workout. None of them had flashed a gun yet, so must've had orders to take Sophia alive.

And that one saving grace was all I needed.

"More of them downstairs. We gotta go," I repeated to Sophia through raspy vocal cords. This time she was ready to heed my warning. At least the remaining tracking device rested at the bottom of the neon-lit pool.

Could hear the police sirens now. Probably from the station over on Seventeenth Street and Convention Center Drive. Less than a mile away, so their response time was to be expected. The conscious one downstairs would either be scared off by them or on his way up toward us to retrieve his partner.

More of the hotel's staff had gathered round. Had all three of us circled nice and tight. A thin pole of a man in a pinstriped suit spoke for all of them.

"We need all of y'all to come downstairs . . . to the office. Need to file a report. The police will get everybody's version. And can sort this shit out," he said with marked irritation in his eyes. With a snap of his fingers, he was gone to handle whatever VIPs needed their dicks polished.

Sophia helped me to my feet. Steadied me while I coughed out the remaining pool water, her eyes thanking me for having her back (again) as we trailed the majority of the hotel staff in search of answers. A sufficient number of them were between us and the prince's *Head Monster in Charge.*

"Remember what happened in Monaco? In the end?" I asked Sophia, as I motioned for her to slow her pace even more. Then I looked past her at something. Waited for her to look as well.

"Yeah? So?" she replied quizzically, the final memory of Jason North coming to mind. Then, catching my drift, she gasped, "You're not saying . . . We can't do that. You almost drowned just now."

"So," I mumbled. "Cops coming. Much worse if we get taken into custody. Go. Check it out."

I stumbled a few steps then bent over, hacking up some more to distract our escorts while Sophia snuck a peek over the balcony that we were passing. When she nodded without that much confidence, I made the next move.

"He's got a gun!" I yelled out, pointing at the big sumo who lumbered in front of me. Just now realized that he was Polynesian, Tongan maybe. Hotel staff already stressed, some rushed him while others scampered for cover.

Just as me and Sophia took three steps to the side.

And hurled ourselves over the side of the glass balcony railing.

For a moment, we hung suspended in air. Daring to fly, but doomed to failure just like Jason North's already lifeless body back in Monaco all those years ago. Arms and legs flailing as we rushed toward the hotel's second level below, it was a relief nothing sharp or protruding waited for us. Nevertheless, this was going to hurt. I kept Sophia as close to me as I could, letting my body take the brunt of the fall as we slammed into sunshades, umbrellas, and several glass tables beneath us.

Came to rest with a stabbing pain in my lower back. Broken glass was beneath me and Sophia lay atop me. Her lovely mouth agape; still in shock and afraid to move. Above by the pool area, I could hear the commotion as our pursuer probably made his move as well. Imagined his large heft flying over the rail and squishing us like bugs. When it didn't come, I was relieved.

"C'mon. Up," I grunted, spurring Sophia into action again. Getting back on our feet, we ran for what we hoped was our final drop. Off the retaining wall, we leaped. Fell more controlled this time knowing what lay below. The two of us slid down an awning before landing beside a couple who were fucking like beasts on the beach. We didn't stay around long enough to disturb their groove or admire the woman's bouncing implants, for I was already dragging Sophia by the arm through the sand for a serious sprint.

We swiftly trudged north along the coastline, a map of the area in my head, guiding me past the distractions and attractions of beach chairs, merengue, couples, and tourists. Every five minutes or so, we'd stop on the dime, giving me time to assess our surroundings or look for a pattern. Patterns, or the absence of them, spoke to me. Sophia knew how I was when I got like this. Knew not to gripe or question.

For I'd proven to be a survivor far too many times.

Three hotels up, we scampered from the beach over the wall into their parking garage. Told Sophia to keep her head low so as to avoid any later ID by the security cameras. Casually, we strolled through the garage, me in a damp suit and she in a bikini top and sarong, while pretending to look for our car. I found one on the employee level in the form of a raggedy old Dodge pickup. Not the nicest option, but an easy one to steal. I removed my jacket, wrapped it around my arm, and promptly busted out the door window.

Before jumping in, I ditched my dress shirt then tore loose a sleeve from it.

"Here," I said as I tossed the makeshift rag underhand at Sophia. "Put your hair up and wrap it with this. Need to change up a little. Look like we belong in this truck."

Coming to the parking garage exit of the Hotel Soku, we rammed the security arm rather than slowing down to pay or risking interaction with someone. With Sophia holding on for dear life, I maneuvered the rocking, rusting husk of a truck onto Collins Avenue to take A1A away from the area.

"Whooo! Just like old times!" Sophia cheered as she looked back at the scattered traffic honking madly at us from our near miss with them.

But that was her.

The wild, fiery risk taker to my cold, calculating self.

"Thank you . . . again," she allowed herself to say as we came to a red light by Bal Harbour, trying to pretend all was normal. "I . . . I don't know how they found us," she mumbled as she allowed her weary head to touch the truck's worn, peeling headrest.

"You're being tracked. That's how," I said gruffly, allowing my anger to bubble up. I checked the rearview mirror, searching for the Audi with diplomatic plates or anyone else who might be in pursuit. Nothing. Yet. "Want to tell me why they want you so bad?" I asked as I shifted the old truck, straining its gears to move through the light that was now green. Knew I should've left South Florida when I had the chance.

"I dunno," she replied, busy pretending to admire the Trump Grand in the distance up the road. As if she hadn't seen more opulent places in her lifetime. Wanted her to be honest. Instead, she remained opaque. Should've left her, just like this state, when I had the chance.

"Talk," I prodded. Even more sternly this time.

"I said, 'I dunno,'" she repeated.

Thinking back to the trackers being used at the hotel, I asked, "What did you bring with you from that place?"

“Nothing. Shit. When you sprung me, I didn’t have a chance to grab anything.”

“Not even earrings or a necklace or something?”

“What part of ‘No’ don’t you get? I was completely naked when we left. Remember?”

“Yeah,” I replied. Not that I believed her. I still gave her lovely body a once-over. Nothing obvious to my eye. “Still . . . they’re tracking you somehow.”

“What do we do then?”

In response, I made a sudden U-turn on Collins Avenue then turned into the parking lot of a 7-Eleven on our right. We were in Sunny Isles Beach now. Maybe we had an hour or two, maybe minutes.

“I need to check you,” I said as I turned the radio off. Just as the rapper Pitbull was saying his call phrase, “*Dale!*”

“You heard him,” Sophia teased. “*Dale.* Hit it. Let’s go. If you’re gonna check me for hidden objects, might as well make it fun. Give ’em a show inside the store.”

She turned toward me, sliding across the dingy bench seat until our bodies contacted one another. Remembered a similar seduction back when Sophia was pretending to be something she wasn’t. And as she leaned over, coming face-to-face with me, her back to the steering wheel, that didn’t make me any less reluctant to play her game for a moment.

Didn’t stop me from kissing her. Plunging my tongue between her parted lips. And tasting her thrills once again.

She placed my hands on her exposed stomach, letting me feel there first. Without finding anything and before I lingered too long, she moved them up to her sides. Still nothing felt other than the tingles her flesh gave me. I moved my hands inward, traipsing lazily over the curves of her breasts. The only objects I found there were hidden no more. I stayed there awhile, her moans goading me as I massaged and pinched her hardened nipples between my fingers. Our kisses grew, a fire threatening to ignite the truck's cabin. From her lips, I moved to her ear, blowing in it softly while tracing the edges with my tongue.

"Mmm. That's it. I want to fuck you so bad, Truth. Right now."

"No. Not now. They might be coming," I responded, fighting to get back on track.

"The only one I'm thinking about coming right now . . . is you," she stressed.

Sophia began pulling on my undershirt, kissing me on my chest as she threatened to go down on me. As I opened my eyes, I spied something peculiar. With her hair up, I could now see a tiny tattoo at the base of her neck.

"When did you get this?" I asked.

"The prince. Gave us all one. Why?" she asked, annoyed by my questions when she had dick on her mind.

I felt over the inked area with my fingers this time . . . as Sophia began unbuckling my belt. Two people inside the 7-Eleven could see the top of Sophia's head and were joking among themselves.

"Stop," I ordered softly. There was something there. Had to be. I pulled Sophia back up, looked her dead in the eyes. "There's something in there. And I need to cut it out. Now," I stated intently.

"Huh? Like hell!" she said, slapping my hand away from her neck.

"Look. You're being tracked. Not me. I can leave you if you want. But they will find you again. Soon."

"And I said you ain't cuttin' on me. Look . . . Get me to a hospital."

"And tell them what? And what if they find us before we make it to a hospital?"

"Then I'll just take my chances. Go. You sprung me, so I can't be mad."

Inside the truck, I looked behind the seat. Found a set of jumper cables. Something in mind, I started the truck back up then got out, raising the hood.

"Need a hand?" one of the men from inside the convenience store asked as he stuck his head out the door.

"Nah. I got this," I replied to the disheartened wannabe Good Samaritan. He went back inside to continue his conversation with the store attendant while Sophia joined me outside the truck.

She walked slowly, cautiously toward me at first. Probably afraid I'd pull out a knife from somewhere and jam it in her neck. As I clamped down one end of the jumper cable pincers on the truck's battery terminals, she remarked, "I thought you used those when you had a dead battery."

"Right," I stated, clacking the other two ends together. Black and red lines touching resulted in a cascade of sparks at my command. That clock was still ticking in my head. We were only mere miles away from our pursuers. And I didn't know the range on the remaining trackers I was sure they had.

"Sooo?" Sophia mumbled, trying to read my face.

Before she could react, I quickly grabbed her with one arm. Held her as she protested and squirmed to get free. "I'm sorry," I uttered to her before placing the red and black clamps together on her neck.

It was ever so briefly. But still enough for her to scream to holy hell from both the emotional and physical jolt she was experiencing. Could feel her body twitching as the truck's current passed through her. After counting down a few seconds, but what seemed like an eternity, I let her go. Jumper cables dropped onto the parking lot as she staggered a few steps away, but no farther. Her muscles were still twitching from their signals being jumbled. Probably felt worse than a Taser.

I rushed to catch her in case she fell. Held her shuddering body close as I whispered in her ear. "I'm sorry. I'm sorry. I had to do it," I pled. "Talk to me."

"You . . . you . . . son of a bitch," she stuttered as tears ran down her face.

"Yeah," I calmly answered. "You're okay?"

"Did it work?" she asked. "Did you get it?"

"Probably," I said. "Needed enough juice to be certain."

"Good," she said as she exhaled heavily. "'Cause if you do something like that again, I'll rip your nuts off with a rusty butter knife."

"Fine. You can have my nuts later. But now let's get back to the room. I have a backup phone and some of my gear I need to grab. Then we're on the next plane outta here."

Just as I slammed the hood shut on the truck, a group of black motorcycles with riders equally shrouded in black zoomed up Collins Avenue, their motors on full rev. Followed by a slower-moving black Audi sedan. I cut my eyes at Sophia.

She'd seen it too.

Looked more afraid at the sight of them than of my impromptu shock session. It wouldn't be long before they realized the signal was lost. And would double back.

Right about here.

"Is everything all right out here? Trouble with your truck?" the man inside the store asked, fully out the 7-Eleven's door this time. "Or with your girl?" he added after a pause.

"Uh . . . yeah, it's all good, *mane,*" I said, adopting a Spanglish accent to make him think I was recently in this country. Luckily, he wasn't paying much attention before. "Me and my girl was jus' playin' 'round and she got shocked. But that truck there is a piece of shit. My brother Manny? He promise to fix the transmission and it go poof," I spat, feigning disgust at the vehicle that wasn't even mine. "You think you can give me and my girl a ride back to the hotel? We want to party some more."

Just then, as his eyes trailed to Sophia, she turned up her sexiness—eyelashes batting, hips wiggling 'n' all. As he stayed fixated on her, I placed my hand firmly on his shoulder. "You wan' to party wid us?" I asked, a foul chuckle escaping me that I didn't know I had.

5

We arrived back at the Crowne Plaza in Sunrise courtesy of our new wheels. Had left our unfortunate Good Samaritan laid out in a Dumpster behind a Publix supermarket in Hialeah on the way here.

"You know the routine. Blow and go. I'll give you five minutes," I yelled, activating my backup cell phone as Sophia freshened up and changed in the bathroom. "The block is hot down here. Gonna switch our flight to an airport farther north. Maybe Orlando or Tampa," I called out as I retrieved my travel app on the phone to rearrange our exodus.

But she didn't comment. All I heard was the rushing water from the shower.

So much for this taking only five minutes.

I sighed. Decided to wash my face in the sink rather than venture within five feet of her. I turned the tap, felt the stream come out warm then adjusted it until it was at its coldest setting. Then I closed the drain, waiting until the sink was filled to the top. I set my backup phone on the counter then plunged my face beneath the water. I stayed there, counting the seconds as the cold revived me. Was difficult putting it out of my head that I'd almost drowned back at that pool, but I still kept my face submerged.

When I withdrew my head from the sink and came up for air, it took a moment to refocus my sight. Took a washcloth to my face and wiped my eyes. And in that moment, I knew I wasn't alone. In the mirror, as I lowered the towel, I saw a blurry form standing behind me. Silent. Must've been hiding in the closet. They'd probably tracked us to the hotel first. Then, finding some of my gear, left someone behind on the off chance that we'd return.

I felt the stabbing pains that racked my body first. Kidney punch. When my legs buckled, he bounced my head a single time against the same sink where I'd been dunking my face. Felt something crack in my nose. Then before I could call out or react, he yanked me backward.

My feet went skyward as the back of my head slammed into the cheap hotel carpet with immense force. With him fast atop me and possessing all the leverage, I saw he wore a tailored suit like the others. A stylish death sent to claim me. From the sudden, abrupt ferocity of the moves, guessed he knew Krav Maga. Never got around to learning it. Not that it mattered. I was weary and outclassed.

As I flailed along on the floor, trying best to block his vicious attack, he rained down harsh elbow strikes to my midsection. Hurt like a motherfucker and got me to lower my guard. Finally knocking the wind out of me, he then delivered a sweeping elbow strike to my temple. Dazed, I fought back. Brought a leg up to kick him in his head, he easily blocked it with his forearm. Then he snagged my ankle, twisting it to where I almost yelped in pain.

I was sloppy. And he'd broken me down easily. As he jumped back to his feet, he clocked me with the butt of his newly revealed pistol to further keep me in check. Wanted me alive to know I was powerless.

That I was beaten.

That he could do whatever he wanted.

As he stood over me, I reached out to the nearby table leg to pull it over. Warn Sophia of what awaited her outside the bathroom. But he placed the silencer-tipped pistol to my forehead and smirked as I froze.

"Call her in here. Like normal. No surprises or maybe I decide not to listen. And neither of you leave this place." English was his second . . . or maybe third language, but there were no communication problems. I was no longer the wildcard like I was back at the hotel. He planned to kill me once he had Sophia in hand.

"Aswad, could you come see?" I calmly called out just as the shower finished running. Since she was known only by that name to him, he failed to recognize the significance of it.

I was warning her.

After a moment of silence, nothing happened, except the barrel of the gun being pressed more firmly into my head.

"Aswad?" I called out again.

"I'm comin', I'm comin'," she growled, finally emerging from the bathroom.

To my surprise, she was fully clothed. A plain olive-green top and matching bottoms she wore with brown sandals on her feet. Minimal jewelry and her hair tucked beneath a colorful scarf, her eyes hid behind a pair of cheap plastic glasses. Except for the glint in her eyes, her sexiness was down to a negative two. Had her looking like a nondescript tourist. Taught her well.

She gasped when she saw our company. Maybe was too hurried or preoccupied to pick up on my warning by calling her "Aswad." She removed her glasses and bit one of the temple tips as she cautiously eyed the two of us. Focused on the gun the longest. Then my eyes.

"Um . . . okay," she chuckled weakly. "How are we gonna resolve this?"

"He wants you back. And the access to those accounts," the arbiter of my fate told her. First time I'd heard of accounts. A vein in my forehead throbbed.

"That's where you're wrong, Hasan," Sophia said defiantly. She knew him by name. This motherfucker was about to kill me and she was on a first-name basis with him. Another game was afoot. That's why she was dawdling rather than getting the fuck outta here. "The prince has to choose. 'Cause his days of locking me away are over. I thought my friend here proved that."

"How much did you pay this one?" he asked, tapping the gun barrel dismissively across the forehead of *this one* who didn't appreciate it in the least. He didn't know much about me. Thought I was just a simple pawn of Sophia's. Maybe he was right.

"Doesn't matter how much I paid him," she replied. "He got results. Unlike you."

"I told you to give me time. I . . . I was going to free you," he stammered. The skilled fighter found himself fumbling in Sophia's ring.

"Fuck you!" she said, letting loose a swift slap that startled me almost enough to make a move on Hasan. But I waited. Wanted to see this play out a bit longer as I caught my breath and got over the smarting from my worked-over body.

"They radioed me before you returned. Said they lost your signal," he said smoothly as if her slap were too insignificant to acknowledge. Finger was still resting on the trigger though. "I haven't told them I found you. Yet," he teased.

And that's what I needed to hear.

His gun didn't move. But I did. Jerked my head aside as fast as I could. When he squeezed the trigger, the shot rang out, barely missing me. As he tried to fire again, I grasped his other wrist and yanked him downward toward me as I leapt up. Suddenly off balance, he wasn't prepared for the jarring motion on his arm and shoulder. Spinning my hips, I brought my left leg up and wrapped it over the back of his neck, cinching my thigh against his carotid artery. On the other side, I clamped my right leg over my left ankle to complete the triangle choke. With his head and shoulder pinned, I yanked on his head with my free hand, pulling it even closer to me. As he tugged to free himself, I held on while struggling with one arm to keep his gun hand angled away from me. Trying to catch me off guard, he tried to roll out of the submission move, but only found himself cinched in tighter to the prison formed by my legs.

"Get . . . the gun!" I yelled at Sophia as she stood, frozen with panic and indecision. Didn't know how much longer I could get by choking him with only one hand available to hold him. When she went to bend over to reach for the pistol, the man she called Hasan must've sensed it. I could keep him from angling it toward me, but when he twisted his wrist away I was unable to stop him from aiming at her. Fortunately, Sophia saw it as well and dove aside. His next shot missed her, striking the hotel wall instead.

I strained my leg muscles, hoping for some sign of him quitting as we continued our struggle on the hotel floor. Then I felt it. That sudden lack of fight in his body as the decreased blood flow to his brain kicked in. He knew it was almost over as well. I just wish it had come sooner.

A final shot rang out before he lost consciousness, the gun finally slipping from his grasp after the discharge. Sophia scampered over on her knees, quickly snatching up the weapon. Just to be certain, I kept the triangle choke applied a full minute longer. Can't say I wasn't worried that Sophia might try to put a bullet in my head while vulnerable.

When I released my chokehold, Hasan slumped over then spilled onto the floor beside me.

And my worries about Sophia seemed more apt than ever.

She grabbed a pillow from off the bed and came over. Looked down at both her potential victims without revealing her intentions. Then, her decision made, she dropped the pillow atop the face of the unconscious Hasan.

Just before emptying the remainder of the clip into the pillow, killing its intended target beneath with an absence of splatter.

Gun at her side and still smoking, but not pointed at me, Sophia nudged her former bargaining partner with her foot just to be certain of the results. "When did you learn to be so flexible with your legs, Kung Fu Panda?" she joked, smiling as if she'd just bought an ice cream rather than having committed murder.

"Research for one of my jobs," I replied, recalling a prior dangerous circumstance in my life, as I tried to take to my feet. But a sudden searing pain in my side halted my progress. Must've been from the kidney punch he'd inflicted or one of our falls we'd taken when fleeing the hotel back at South Beach.

"Are you okay?" Sophia asked as she helped me up.

"Yeah, I'm fine," I said, taking to my feet. But after one step, I knew I wasn't. Adrenaline had masked it.

Now the intense burn was evident followed by the dizziness I was experiencing.

"Oh Lord!" she gasped uncharacteristically. Her eyes drew my attention to my side. In the end, Hasan had gotten lucky with his final try. A circled pool of crimson had soaked through my shirt from underneath.

And it was growing.

I'd been shot.

Sophia was pacing at the foot of the bed when I came to. I didn't let her know I'd awakened as she mumbled something to herself. Looked as if she'd been crying. If I remembered correctly, we were at Westside Regional Medical Center. Recalled a series of red lights whizzing by on Broward Boulevard, all the while Sophia's voice repeating that she was sorry.

We had to scramble to the nearest hospital before I bled out. Sophia cooked up the story that we were robbed and that I got beaten and shot when I tried to protect her. Story would hold for now. But we'd left a mess back at the hotel. No time for clean up if I wanted to live. Between that and the fiasco down in South Beach, someone was going to connect tonight's dots. Especially once my gunshot was reported by the hospital to the authorities.

Was hard to focus through the haze of medication following my emergency surgery. Face was swollen, too, causing me discomfort when I moved my jaw. The lights seemed to flicker in and out. But I knew it was just me.

"Why does the prince want you back so bad? What do you have of his?" I asked her, announcing my return to the waking world. She quickly turned her back to me so as to wipe her eyes. When she turned back around, the façade was in place—a big-ass smile and doe-eyed relief. "No bullshit or subterfuge this time," I stressed wearily before any bullshit or subterfuge could escape her lips. "What . . . do . . . you . . . have . . . of . . . his?"

"Access," she replied coldly. "He pissed me off when he wouldn't let me go. So I gained access to several of his accounts one night. Changed passcodes 'n' shit. Froze him out and put them under my control."

"What . . . what's in those accounts?" I pushed, while trying to reposition myself in the bed and paying the price in pain.

"Money. Money transfers . . . 'n' stuff," she offered, her voice trailing off as I struggled to remain conscious. Had to think. But was so hard.

"Stuff," I repeated, chuckling lazily. Stuff to a powerful man like him was much different than what ordinary folk kept under wraps. Nothing silly like photos of his dick or porn. The prince probably had secrets that could bring governments down. Or that governments wanted. No wonder he'd tagged Sophia with a tracking chip.

And she kept me in the dark. Had me flying blind while she stuck around town in the hopes of working a side deal and still cashing in.

The nurse, a tall glass of chocolate Bahamian goodness, entered the room. She smiled in my direction, but seemed less than thrilled with Sophia. They'd probably sparred while I was in recovery. "Ma'am," she said, "your husband needs his rest. And I need you to complete the insurance information up front. Also, the police need to speak with you about the assault on your husband."

"Can you give us a moment? Please. Then I promise to rest," I asked of the nurse, mustering a smile as best I could. With some consternation, she agreed.

"I know what you're about to say. And I'm not leaving," Sophia said as she sat at my side. She placed her fingers across my lips as she rested her head next to mine.

"Yes, you are," I said, moving her hand aside. "You don't owe me anything."

"I . . . I'm not leaving. We're like magic together. And it's been too long. You're going to need me now more than ever," she countered, that voice of hers dropping an octave. Now it was getting weird in here. Sophia's irrational need to have a man controlling her. Could be me this time. Other times, the prince. Or someone else from her past.

Thing is, I would never trust her. Especially after this fiasco.

"Ivan's free," I offered succinctly. An arrow always notched in my bow and ready for release, this one sprang free. Found its target. You just have to know where to aim and when to strike.

"What?" Sophia asked as she suddenly flinched. She backed away enough to look me in my puffy, bruised face. I wouldn't believe me either.

"Ivan's free," I repeated, striking her with the name of the man responsible for her first stint in jail. A man she'd once admitted she'd do anything for. Her first love, as delusional as it was. I continued while still lucid, "Released from prison last month. Word is he's looking for you, too."

"So," she said with a shrug. "That's been over. I'm my own woman now."

"It was only over as long as he was behind bars. But now he's free. Aren't you happy? Didn't he used to make you cum like no other?" I asked, reflecting on a once truth for her that she'd revealed.

"Stop being a bastard."

"Hurting people's my specialty. Remember?"

"Yeah. Because you left your poor broken heart back in Dallas. And probably your nuts, too," she retaliated with a grenade to my arrow. Even threw in a fake boo-hoo sob face to further irk me. "Since you can't pretend to be an author anymore, do you still spy on her like a lovesick little boy?"

"Don't go there," I said. "Look. Cops are comin'. And you went and *bodied* someone back at the hotel. Doubt this ends good. So just go."

"As much as you've pissed me off, I can't leave you like this."

"I'll be fine. Work better on my own anyway. Now go. You got time to drive to Tampa for that flight."

I shut my eyes, letting the medicine take hold. Easier that way as our partings were usually more acrimonious. When I opened them again, Sophia had gone.

"Sir, where is your wife?" my nurse asked as she returned to the room, half expecting to argue with a defiant Sophia. Instead she got only me. Minus Sophia's static, had a chance to study her some more. "The police want to speak with her," she said as she checked her watch and then pulled back my sheet to observe my wound. When she did, I took her hand.

"Can I let you in on a secret?" I asked her, summoning my strength to appear more coherent as I gazed into her engaging brown eyes.

"Yes," she replied, somehow still drawn to me despite my rough circumstances. I smiled appreciatively.

"Y'see . . . that woman's not my wife. And you're not going to believe what I'm about to tell you," I spun in her willing ear as I leaned in.

And with that, I had my way out of here as I began concocting a story that would ensure her cooperation to help me escape the hospital . . . and the police.

For I am not only Proteus, wearer of many forms . . .

I'm Loki, trickster and teller of many lies.

6

A Month Ago
The Bronx

I waited for the NYPD cruiser to turn onto Roosevelt Avenue then began waving my arms. I was sure they were tired of seeing me. I'd become a fixture on the streets around here, offering to do odd jobs and storefront window washing in exchange for money, meals, or whatever.

"Yo, you got some change, my man?" I asked of the officer as he pulled curbside.

"What for?" he asked, rolling his eyes at his partner who seemed bored with the day's routine.

"Wanna get somthin' from Latin Kitchen. A nice meal for a change. Maybe meet a pretty lady, y'know," I replied with a shitty grin from behind the false teeth meant to look like I was missing a few of my own.

The officer shook his head while looking at his partner. "Don't think they're gonna let you in there with the way you're dressed . . . or the way you smell. Bro, you got nothin' better to do than hustle on this corner? Don't make me pick you up for harassing people," he admonished while slipping me a dollar bill. Ronnie Dexter was his name. He'd been on the force for five years. Married with two kids. But was fucking this Dominican hairdresser over at Sophie's Set & Style on Tremont Avenue.

"I'm harmless, my man. No worries, no hassles."

"Keep it that way. Seen anything we should know about?" Officer Dexter asked. Anything from 5-0, even if just a dollar, came at a price.

"Nope. And that's why I like it around here. Nice friendly folk. No trippin' off a brother down on his luck," I answered. "Did I tell you about when I was in the army? Could tell you some stories 'bout chaos."

"Yeah, yeah. You told us alllll about that," he said, cutting me off. "Think about getting your life together, my man. Okay?"

"Next time I'm at the V.A. hospital, I'ma ask 'em ta help me with that, Officer Dexter," I said with a subservient bow of my head.

The squad car left me to make its rounds, which included a left turn that would take them in front of a certain Dominican beauty shop. I'd barely stepped back onto the curb when I bumped into a passerby. Far from the talkative sort, he carried a grocery bag from the corner deli and meat market.

"Excuse me, sir. Got any change you can spare? Jus' wanna get a bite to eat. No alcohol or nothin', I promise," I spit out before he could get clear of me. I say spit out because I literally was hurling spit through my misshapen teeth.

"Yeah, yeah. Here," he said, hastily digging in his pocket to fish for loose change. When he couldn't find any, he gave me a dollar. Now I'd made two in less than ten minutes. Maybe there was a career for me in panhandling after all.

"Thank you, sir. I sho do appreciate that," I said, grinning wildly again at the short man who wanted nothing more than to get back inside his basement apartment and quietly hole up below ground for another week. He wore a cheap black wig and an even cheaper orange spray tan coated his skin, his face two shades darker than his hands. This is what his life had come down to.

Running into me in the Bronx.

Two of us out here pretending to be something we weren't.

Except for me; this was my life—deception and mistruths.

Looking over my shoulder, I staggered down the street talking to myself. When I got to Tremont, I retrieved a pristine Bluetooth from my dirty, worn pockets and placed it in my ear. From the tattered jacket I wore, I pulled out a cell phone that looked like I'd stolen it. I dialed the single number programmed in and removed my false teeth to speak more clearly.

"Put him on the phone," I said to the exotic feminine voice that answered. Followed that up with a few coughs to clear my throat. Had been talking in that raspy manner for so long that my own vernacular and tone felt foreign. Like I had to learn to be me again.

Whoever that was.

"He's sparring. May I ask whose calling?"

"No. He'll know. He's been waiting." Of course he was. This number was only to be used by me and him. Per my instructions from the day I took this job.

Over a month ago.

God, I needed a shower.

Followed by a nice distraction of the female kind.

After a delay of about a minute, he came to the phone. Just when I was about to hang up. Couldn't risk a sudden change of heart or a trace of this call.

"Took you long enough. Thought you'd run off with my money. Shit like that don't come easy," Arturo

Diaz, the world's reigning welterweight champion from Spanish Harlem, remarked in a winded manner.

"You know better than that. Results take time."

"So you found the right car?"

"Yep. Black minivan. Just like you wanted. Didn't have to go out of town, either."

"For real?"

"*Sí*. Right across the Throgs Neck Bridge."

"Shit," he mouthed in almost a whisper. "You found it in the Bronx? On that end? I'll be damned. You sure you can't just—"

"No. What you paid me was a finder's fee. I found the right one. I'll leave the customization to you."

"Where in the Bronx?"

"Get your detail people on the road now. Have them ready to pick it up. When I hang up, I'll text you the address and all you need. It's dusty, so I'd stay away personally if I were you. Let them fix it up while you keep on sparring for your big fight. You wouldn't want to be seen in a minivan anyway."

"You did it. You fuckin' did it," he muttered with a deep sigh. "Thank you, man. I—"

Time was up for the call. On the line too long. And no need getting all mushy over what was going to be far from sweet and sentimental.

But retribution rarely is.

A black minivan was our code. Black for the color of death or a hearse. Minivan . . . for something associated with kids.

Larry Roth, the man hiding out here on the southeast side of the Bronx, was infamous. Had kidnapped Arturo's little sister last year. Around the same time as I was getting shot down in Florida because of Sophia. Anyway, Roth kept her in a hidden room in his basement for over a week. The bastard raped her repeatedly until, one day, she miraculously escaped. Made the news even where I was convalescing in the Bahamas. Most thought he'd fled into Canada through upstate New York. Not long after all legit leads on Larry dried up, I got the call. People knew how to get in touch with me . . . or rather the person or persons they thought I was. Few know the true me.

And as one in my past found out, to truly know me is to hate me.

I'm paid to destroy people's lives, but this job was slightly different.

A life had already been destroyed by that monster back there, a white man pretending to be a brown man so as to hide in plain sight. Desperate, depraved motherfucker.

Who knows how many others had run into him before Arturo's sister?

No child was safe.

They were the only ones worth saving.

I would've done this job for free.

Maybe.

But one month's work for a cool million upfront wasn't too shabby.

I texted Arturo the address where Larry Roth was hidden, completing my end of the deal. His people would swoop in to exact revenge for innocence stolen and the world would be none the wiser that a sick man no longer dwelled among the living.

From out of a nearby storm drain, I fetched a waterproof bag I'd stowed that held a pair of Under Armour running shoes. An idiosyncrasy I'd developed in the town that gave me my name. Had been caught off guard that time in the desert. Had to run for my life barefooted. A bad time.

But never again.

Ditching my old, worn props, I quickly donned the comfortable shoes then set off on my trek, the neighborhood bum suddenly darting and dashing like someone ten years his junior. I ran as fast as I could, taking a shortcut through Saint Raymond's Cemetery en route to the Public Self Storage on Bush Avenue. Inside one of their prepaid storage units, a motorcycle, ID, and change of clothes awaited.

And just like Larry Roth, a cheery, snaggletoothed homeless man would never be seen again after today either.

For not only was I patient.

I was prepared.

7

Freshly shaven and sporting a designer suit, I walked briskly through Midway. I'd just touched down in Chicago from Newark and taken a cab over from O'Hare. Another airline, another identity. While heading toward my gate for the Southwest flight to Oakland, I reached into my jacket pocket. Sifted through my multiple SIM cards and retrieved the carefully marked one I was looking for. Not breaking my stride, I switched it to my other pocket where I swapped it out with a different SIM card inside my cell.

When I stopped to review the overhead departure schedule, I placed a call.

"Yo. Who this?" Francis Martin Quinones, the head valet attendant at the Stratus hotel in Las Vegas, answered. Two hours ahead, so probably hadn't left for work yet.

"Uptown callin'," I replied, donning the voice I used whenever I dealt with him. Francis not only funneled business my way, like he did with the Arturo Diaz job, but had helped me on a previous job in Vegas. Dude really thought I was from Harlem. And with him being from Queens by way of the Bronx, it didn't hurt to keep up the illusion.

"Hey! What's goin' on, my man?" Frankie the valet enthusiastically responded. "Thought something had happened to you 'n' shit."

Ignoring his concern, I pressed on. "Nah. I'm good. Hey. That key I left you. Greyhound bus station on South Main. Locker number 237. Got it?"

"No shit?"

"Yeah. I'm serious. A token of appreciation. You deserve it for makin' that connect. Looks like you might be outta the valet business, son."

"Furreal? Thank you! Thank you! Thank you for takin' this job. You's a bad motherfucka, yo! Off top! We need ta go out fer drinks or somethin', my man. Or at least let me take ya to the strip club. When you comin' back to Vegas?"

As I approached my next gate, and too many nearby ears, I wrapped up the love fest. "Thanks, but I got some other work to put in right now. Gonna have to catch you later."

Something had me feeling off though. Years of instincts built up like a scab, but couldn't put my finger on it. Bothered me enough that I stopped in the restroom, rechecking my ID in the stall and ensuring no followers before exiting.

Confident that my shit was tight, I joined the group of flyers waiting for their rows to be called. Could've easily left the airport and snagged a rental car instead. Just me and the open road with Sirius XM if I so chose. But my sudden departure may have attracted unwanted attention that I'd only imagined until this point. All I had to do now was to breathe easy and enjoy the flight to Oakland. Then a drive up I-5 to Seattle and it would be all good.

"First time flying?" the middle-aged businessman shuffling beside me asked in his even Midwestern cadence. The witty flight attendant on the mic had just called the group ahead of me. By the way we were both hovering, letting others move in front, he probably was boarding next as well.

"No. Have a sick aunt in Tennessee who's on my mind," I replied on a whim. Damn me for letting someone try to read my mind. Must've stood out by my body language.

"Oh. I am so sorry," he offered, feeling sufficiently bad for intruding on my conflicted thoughts. "Didn't mean to be all in your business."

"That's quite all right, sir," I replied, a bit of Southern drawl creeping in now as the flight attendant called on our batch of seats for boarding.

Found my way easily to an empty seat in row fifteen. Seat C. After stowing my single carry-on bag in the overhead, I hung my noise-cancelling headphones around my neck. Prepared for whenever we'd be free to use approved electronic devices. Except, as ordinary as mine looked, with a flip of the switch in the opposite direction, mine would amplify external sounds through its microphone rather than muffle them. Spying on others' conversations while I pretended to sleep was always an amusing distraction. For you never know when a borrowed portion of someone else's life might be of use.

No one else was seated next to me, giving me an unobstructed view of the tarmac as the cabin doors shut and we were told to turn off our phones. Once the plane cleared the gate, I finally eased back into my seat, letting the tension ebb from my muscles as some clumsy freestyle explaining the different ways to kiss your ass good-bye in the event cabin pressure was lost blared over the intercom. After a delay of several minutes, we began taxiing for takeoff. Oakland and a rental car under yet another name awaited me.

The woman seated in the row in front of me made the sign of the cross then closed her eyes, a silent prayer for a safe flight no doubt. While she relied on her beliefs, I focused on my belief in myself. Discretely counted the number of passengers along with the flight attendant who, when finished, quickly scurried to her seat in the front of the plane for takeoff. The rev of the engines as we entered onto the runway for takeoff, led me to don my headphones.

Then, just as the plane entered onto the final runway for takeoff, their power was cut.

"Aww, what the fuck?" an older man at the back of the plane with zero patience blurted out. The random groans throughout the cabin were in agreement.

"'Wanna get away,' my ass," someone else with a sense of humor added. I removed my headphones, expecting some news.

And it came.

"Uh . . . ladies and gentlemen, this is your captain speaking," the monotone voice rumbled over the plane's intercom system. "I sincerely apologize for the delay, but our flight has been diverted momentarily for further screening. Nothing to be alarmed about and I'm sure everything will be done to assure we're back on our way as soon as possible and that all connections in Oakland are made. Thank you in advance for your cooperation and patience."

Announcement made me check my boarding pass yet again. Pretended I was worried about missing a connection when I really just making sure my role was memorized for whatever was to come. The plane moved along at a mechanical crawl, coming to a maintenance hangar where law enforcement vehicles and airport equipment surrounded the exterior. Some of the other passengers saw this too and began panicking. Whispers about terrorist plots beginning to percolate as the stepped-up security rattled them. At the front of the cabin, I watched the head flight attendant receive her orders via radio, nodding to whatever she was hearing. As I began keying in on the exit doors, I also watched for something unusual from my fellow passengers that I'd taken for granted. Maybe it was just the bags that needed to be rescreened, but I doubted it.

The main cabin door opened, allowing a single TSA agent to come aboard. He met with the captain first then explained further what the flight attendants needed to do. No guns were drawn. Maybe something minor after all.

"Attention, everyone," she announced. "We'll need y'all to deplane with your bags as you would as if exiting at your destination. Keep in mind that you'll be exiting down a set of stairs, so be careful. Let's keep it orderly so we can be back underway as soon as possible."

When it came time for my row's exodus, I retrieved my carry-on and followed the procession from the plane. When I emerged at the top of the airstairs, I noticed the heightened security below. Two armed men at the bottom and a whole detail separating the passengers into smaller groups that were being wanded with handheld metal detectors while dogs sniffed at their bags.

I descended the stairs into their midst, anxious as to how this shit was going to play out.

"Any idea how long this is going to take?" I asked as I flippantly handed my bag and boarding pass receipt over then checked my watch. "I have a wedding party to attend in Napa and I'm the best man."

"Not too long, sir," the overly polite brother towering over me replied. "And we'll do everything we can to get you back in the air in no time."

One of the TSA workers stood out. He was supposed to be searching another passenger's bag. But his eyes were steady on me from his peripheral vision, while faking a rummage through her Louis Vuitton.

And he looked nervous. Triggered those hairs on the back of my neck as I began calculating how far I could get before they caught me.

Not far by my estimation.

I leaned in toward my handler. Lowered my voice to barely a whisper, hoping to sow chaos once more. "Bro, I didn't want to say this onboard the plane, but . . . I think I heard somebody say something was up with the Middle Eastern man in row thirty. Now I got nothin' against those people, but if there's something wrong on this flight then . . ."

"One-way ticket," he said to himself while perusing my boarding pass. Doing like he was trained. Focus on the thing at hand no matter how much background chatter I was providing. "That's one of our red flags. Sir, if you could just head over there with your bag for further screening, we'll be sure to address any issues there might be with row thirty."

"See that you do," I said as I gave him a firm handshake and walked off. He was right. One-way tickets always commanded more scrutiny since 9/11. At least the office where I was directed might give me more options if I needed to cut and run.

Besides, the one I'd caught eyeing me no longer seemed concerned. Maybe he was just hatin' on a fly brother in a nice suit. Before I turned the knob on the office door, I looked back at the man who'd herded me in this direction. He nodded, urging me on with a smile before inspecting the next person's ticket.

I walked into an office that was absent any TSA or other passengers. From behind an old wooden desk covered in invoices and repair orders, a single person at the far end of the tight space beckoned me deeper. He was a stringy-haired man in a rumpled gray sport coat and black slacks. Looked out of place in the dirty, cluttered surroundings that reeked of oil and hydraulic fluid.

Before any options came to mind, an armed man entered behind me before either of us could exchange pleasantries. His eyes were obscured by black sunglasses and his clothes were missing any markings that would identify him as TSA or law enforcement. He quickly patted me down, removing my phone from my pocket and inspecting it thoroughly as if it might be something other than what it appeared. Then, as he replaced my phone in my pocket, he looked to the man who was probably his boss. Still no words, but his eyebrows rose from behind the sunglasses—their own little language worked out presumably from years together.

The man behind the desk nodded. "Finish up with the screening, then let 'em back in the air," he crowed matter-of-factly. "I got this one." What was it with motherfuckers referring to me as *this one?*

"Excuse me?" I said as I hastily stalked toward the desk he'd obviously appropriated for this sole purpose. "I know my rights as a paying airline customer! And if you're trying to harass me because I'm black—"

"Drop the act and have a seat, son," he said, abruptly cutting me off mid-routine. "'Cause if you even think about trying to run, there's three more just like him waiting on the other side of that door."

Sunglasses grinned at me for a millisecond before reverting to stone and exiting the room.

"And I ain't no terrorist," I snapped, swiftly switching tactics.

"Yeah. You're probably right about that," he responded unfazed as he chose to finally stand. He walked around the desk and came forward, holding a folder in his hand. Was slightly taller than me and had an odd gait as if one of his legs had once been injured. "The question . . . is just what are you," he said from behind a cold, coffee-stained smile.

Whoever he was and whoever he answered to was patient.

Like me.

Waited until I'd boarded the plane with no chance of escape before springing the trap.

"We missed you in Newark by this much," he said, pinching his thumb and index finger together. "Oh, you're a slippery one, ain't cha? But we got you now. We got you now."

8

He stood two feet away, not completely confident in his assessment of me no doubt. I warily looked on as he opened the folder then flipped a photo at my feet.

"I could make you strip, but I think we've seen enough of that," he commented as I looked at the black-and-white photo captured of me au naturel outside the compound down in Florida when I sprang Sophia. "Going to deny it's you? 'Cause whatever is on your boarding pass I'm sure is more bullshit," he taunted. Then he dropped another photo. Like fuckin' playing cards and showing his hand one at a time.

It was the body of that man Hasan lying on the room floor of the Crowne Plaza with a bullet hole through his head.

"Messy," he quipped. Then he dropped another.

This one was of a decomposed body in what looked to be a garbage dump.

I refused to give him the satisfaction of my recognition. But despite its appearance, I recalled the clothes of a man once sent to kill me. It was on an elevator in Dallas. In a place I once considered my sanctuary. Like Hasan, I hadn't physically killed that man either. He died when his partner shot recklessly and missed.

Never knew what had happened to his body until now.

Not that I cared. He'd simply paid for trying to take me out.

"Tell me this," my inquisitor posed, having laid out his preliminary evidence. "How does the murder of an Armenian thug in Dallas years ago connect with your little jailbreak at Prince Abdel Al-Bin Sada's in Miami? I think Dallas PD was looking for someone named Chris Davis back then for that and the kidnapping of a blind girl. Now . . . they never found this person, but his fingerprints happen to match yours we lifted from that Florida hotel. Thing is, there are no other matches in our database. And we have a big database. Huge. It's almost like you don't exist. So . . . tell me. What's your name? The real one, *Chris.*"

"Tell me yours and I'll tell you mine," I taunted back.

"It's no matter," he chimed. "We got video of you while keeping an eye on ol' Princey in our country. Had never seen or heard of you in my circles, but you're obviously a professional. How is that, I wonder? Then *poof* . . . you disappear from under our noses without a trace. At least until our facial recognition software snagged you when boarding in Newark."

"Then how'd you catch me here in Chicago? I switched airports."

He made a whistling sound, pointing to the air. "Duh. Eyes in the sky," he replied.

"You mean like a predator drone? This isn't a warzone. Those things are illegal over here, aren't they?"

"Riiight," he responded. "I didn't say specifically what we used, but we're the U.S. of fuckin' A., son. We do what we want."

I clapped, mocking him. "You're too brilliant for me, jackass."

"Watch your mouth. Since technically we have no record of you, I could throw your ass in Guantanamo and forget all about you."

"You probably don't want me there. Otherwise, I'd be in cuffs and face down on the ground. Not listening to you telling me how powerful and almighty you are."

"A real cocky one, huh? Don't let what you pulled on Prince of the Sand Niggers and his overpriced, underqualified seven dwarfs swell your head, son. You're dealing with true professionals now. Underpaid and battle hardened."

I stopped goading him, but had to show him I still had some fight left. "What do you want? You haven't arrested me yet or read me my rights. And you had the room emptied just for this *talk*. You're certainly not TSA. I would say FBI because of the surveillance on the prince, but from the Bruce Willis act, you're probably a spook," I said, offhandedly referring to the CIA.

"Spook? Such an outdated term. Too many bad late-night movies while Mommy was out whoring or shooting up heroin?" He saw the brief flash of anger, no matter how slight that it was, over his disparaging remarks about my mother. Could tell it amused him, but he moved on. Wanted something from me. "An agreement among gentlemen is what I want. A simple use of your unique talents. That's all," he said as he bent over and retrieved the three photos he'd displayed for dramatic effect. He placed them back inside the folder that contained other items either real or falsified to work on my nerves.

"And what do I get out of such an agreement?" I asked. "Because I don't do pro bono. And despite those pictures, which may or may not have anything to do with me, I'm not a killer."

"I'm offering you freedom, mystery man. The ability to continue to move around this country and probably the world if you want," he replied, trying to fake a warm smile. "And the alternative? I cart you off, photograph and fingerprint you then lock you away. And even if you somehow pull a Criss Angel, I post every scrap of info on you I know on watch lists with every jurisdiction, every airport, every seaport, and every border crossing imaginable. You become hunted for whatever heinous crime I can come up with. And I have a vivid imagination, trust me. Now you seem like a man who values his anonymity. I can guarantee that continues. And that people like Prince Abdel Al-Bin Sada or the Dallas PD or whoever don't suddenly catch wind of your trail again."

My shoulders dropped in defeat. "What do I have to do?" I asked.

"Well. Wasn't expecting you to give up so easily," he admitted, taken aback.

"And I wasn't expecting to get caught," I commented, slowly morphing into a beaten man who would fan the flames of his ego. This guy was used to winning, so it wasn't very hard. Sun Tzu once said, "While strong in reality, appear to be weak; while brave in reality, appear to be cowardly."

He smiled, genuine warmth intruding as he felt at ease enough to share.

For now I would listen.

And when the time was right, it would be my turn to spring a trap.

But first . . . patience.

Patience.

9

"Thought you weren't going to make it back on in time," my fellow passenger, a woman I hadn't particularly noticed when I first boarded back in Chicago, stated as we exited the flight together. But I noticed everyone now. And as fine and sexy as she was, she made it easy to hold my attention. The cute down jacket with fur lining was made for cooler climates giving her that East Coast swagger. Lady Lovely wore her designer jeans with a certain bop of her hips. Like she just *knew* they fit her well and she was expecting high fives from passersby. Her sandals were Louboutins, evident by the signature red bottoms that flashed in the reflection of the terminal windows every few steps.

"I had a one-way ticket, so they decided to search all my stuff. Do I look like a terrorist?" I scoffed as I held my gaze in her eyes longer than necessary for basic conversation. The sister sported an expensive ebony lace front wig that framed her slight, angular face. From her exotic eyes, looked like she may have been mixed with Korean or something. If I had to guess, I'd say she was once a military brat. Straightforward and direct who answered to authority yet mixed with a devilish, rebellious streak.

"No, you don't look like a terrorist at all," she said with a smile meant to make me think she was bashful or modest. "In fact, my opinion of you hasn't changed since I first saw you board. Was going to ask if you wanted some company on your row. Before they halted the flight and yanked us from the plane. After that, I just sat my black ass still and prayed we didn't get de-planed again."

"Definitely would've made it more pleasant, but I understand. Still, I'm glad they didn't find anything. Otherwise I might not be having this conversation with you," I responded, smiling even more.

"Cathy," she said, taking the opportunity to introduce herself as she switched her roller bag trailing behind her to the opposite side. Hand was soft and smooth with French tips on her manicured nails. Kinda wanted to interlock my fingers with hers.

"Russell," I replied off the name on my boarding pass which I'd just dropped in the trash.

"I heard you mention a wedding when we were pulled off the plane. You the groom, Russell?"

"Nah. Not in my future. Single and lovin' it. A friend of mine's the sucker. Wedding's up in Napa. I'm actually early, so wanted to see a little of the Bay Area before that."

"Friends picking you up?"

"No. Solo. Just me and my rental car."

"Could I bother you for a ride then?" she asked, a little less bashful, a little less modest.

"Mmm. Yeah, daddy. Give. Me. That. Dick," Cathy gushed literally and figuratively, heavy on the baby talk while riding me as if she were an accomplished equestrian. As Kelly Rowland's "Motivation" played in the background, I took a swig from the remaining bottle of Louis Roederer then poured some of the bubbly across her chest. Lapped it off her with my tongue then sucked on her bounding breasts as the drops gathered on her taut little nipples.

We were in her suite at the Hilton Garden Inn. Just off the Bay Bridge in Emeryville. She was in town for a music conference, covering it for her urban magazine and Web blog. I decided to stay around, sticking to my role as a simple traveler en route to his boy's wedding. I'd really held off on my drive up to Seattle in case my new client, with all the resources at his disposal, was still having me tracked.

Or if Cathy was not who she appeared to be.

For trust was something I was short on in this world.

Either way, I decided to make the most of my time.

Played all attentive-like while Cathy had shared her thoughts on current R&B from Trey Songz, Ne-Yo, and Chris Brown, comparing it to the singers of the late '80s like Keith Sweat, Al B. Sure!, and Bobby Brown. Had passionately discussed topics ranging from the musical genius of Prince to Jennifer Hudson's weight loss. Even hung out with her while she shopped on Bay Street at places like Bebe and Victoria's Secret, with the promise of her modeling some of it for me later.

After a full day of indulging her music industry commentary and shopping fetish, we'd dined on spring rolls and lettuce wraps at PF Chang's where we came up with the wild idea of champagne and strawberries back at her hotel.

The strawberries, while fresh and tasty, were long gone.

And the champagne wasn't far behind.

With one hand on the bottle, I cupped that ass of which she was so proud then stood up, carrying her with me. Let her wrap her arms around my neck as

I walked to the window while still all up in her moist confines. She tightened her powerful thighs, flexing and releasing them as she cinched up against my waist until our sweaty bodies merged. Felt those passionate lips on my neck as she mumbled, "Damn, I ain't came like this in a long time."

As I stared out at the Golden Gate Bridge and the tiny specks of light dotting it, Cathy resumed slowly riding up and down on my dick. "Don't quit on me now, boy," she purred as another shudder went through her body. Had briefly gone back to my frustration of what had happened in Chicago, but now my full attention returned to her.

Sweet.

Seductive.

Clueless.

I let the almost-empty champagne bottle slip from my grasp. It made a single thunk as it landed on the carpet and rolled away.

Took full hold of her ass as I looked into her eyes and smiled.

"What?" she asked, no doubt curious about the pause of the man she knew as Russell.

I didn't answer, letting my actions speak instead. Pressed her against the window, whose cool touch to her back evoked a startled gasp from her wanting lips.

I engulfed her mouth full on with mine, a chorus of desire rising from us as our breathing built in intensity. I kissed those full, soft lips, sucking heavily on them. Played with her tongue, too, then peppered her neck with a mix of smaller kisses and sharp bites that seemed to delight her to no end. She grasped my face, darting her tongue lazily across my cheek. Then she nipped at my earlobe with her teeth while whispering sweet obscenities of how she needed the dick so bad. Obliging, I pressed Cathy more firmly against the window, fingers digging and finding purchase in handfuls of her ass as I began working my hips in further exploration of her—rocking, winding then plunging with my swollen dick until it filled her. Each thrust deeper inside evoked more and more of her sweet, sticky honey, waves of cum besieging me as I went in and out.

"Shit," I gasped, feeling myself overcome and heading toward the eventual. Instincts moving me into the passing lane where no letup existed until that final crash.

"Uh huh. Don't stop," she said, understanding where our bodies were taking us and egging me on. I carried Cathy away from the window and over to the bed where I dropped her onto the mattress. "How you want it, daddy?" she asked, looking over her shoulder at me then licking her lips over the sight of my hovering dick. She crawled over, licking a bit of her still-moist essence off the head before lingering on the tip where she proceeded to tickle with her tongue. For a brief second, I saw Sophia instead as I shuddered. But feeling the scar on my lower abdomen quickly dispelled that illusion. I motioned for Cathy to turn around and get on her hands and knees then slid my dick in again, taking her from behind. On my first hard thrust deep in them guts, she reached up to make sure her lace front was still secure in place. On my next one, she moaned readily, arching her back to receive me. With each pump, she bumped her ass against me, eagerly accepting my length. With both of us in a groove again, she came even harder. Our bodies slapped together repeatedly, the room air filling with the overpowering aura of our sex as we fucked.

Then as I looked down at that perfect ass of hers and slapped it, I felt it again. The body following its own urges and the need for release that I could only fight for so long. I leaned over and reached to Cathy's front, grasping her breasts as I worked her pussy from behind even more. Pressed harder, firmer up against her ass as any sense of control fled me. Went deeper with my dick throbbing wildly inside her, those primal moans now a spiritual chant as she sat up on her knees, arms writhing up to heaven with me steady fucking her from behind. I was a speeding race car absent a driver as I slipped and slid about, awash in her all.

"Yes, yes," I panted as I kissed her neck.

Cathy, sensing it, flexed her hips even harder, ass cheeks quaking and jiggling with each collision of our bodies as she goaded me to end it.

Then it came.

My senses plunged into disarray as I released my seed in a violent eruption. Reflexes led me to clench her body tighter as we both came, our spasms generating even more sensations between us as we tumbled onto our sides, puppets whose strings were cut at the conclusion of our act. There wasn't enough sex-tinged air in the room for us to breathe as I labored for a moment to get past the black spots before my eyes. Euphoria had given way to beautiful exhaustion.

With us both lifeless and spent naked across the bed, I somehow found enough energy to get up and head to the bathroom. Inside, I removed my condom and discarded it with my DNA down the toilet before splashing some water on my face. Looking up, I glared at that scar once again. The bullet wound, now healed . . . at least physically. When I peeked out, Cathy had settled into a slumber, her eyelids flickering as she breathed with her mouth agape. Wanted nothing more than to lazily join her bliss just then . . . and maybe fuck again later, but other duties were pressing.

I'd snagged her purse.

Inside it, I found a Kentucky driver's license due to expire in three months and several credit cards belonging to a Catherine Yoon-jin Wilson along with some business cards from New York and the Chicago area. All looked to be legitimate.

I'd brought my phone with me in the bathroom and after a quick search, found Cathy's online presence including her Twitter account. I smiled when I found one of her tweets from earlier in the evening.

> @MissMuzak773 Ya girl in Oakland n already found a nice chocolate treat on da flight in. Don't know his name yet, but . . . #YaKnow #BayAreaMusicConf #Winning

When I crept from out of the bathroom, Cathy was stirring. Before she turned over, I placed her purse back on the floor among her discarded clothes.

"You coming back to bed, Russell?" she cooed groggily as she rolled over, seeing me standing there by the light of the bathroom.

"In a minute. I left my wallet down in the car. Don't know this area like that," I said as I quickly threw on my clothes.

"Don't take too long. I'll be ready for another taste of that soon. You the truth, boy," she said, pointing between my legs as she stifled a yawn.

"*What did you say?*" I asked.

"I said, 'you the truth,'" she answered. "What's wrong, babe?"

"Nothin'. Forget about it," I said with a smile, laughing inside at being spooked by her unintentionally saying my real name. "Just keep it warm for me," I taunted, knowing that pussy would be long cold before she ever saw me or my dick again. Shame, but I'd enjoyed the distraction.

Downstairs, I went outside where I was greeted by the cool, damp air. Shit. The temperature had already dropped several degrees from when it was daylight. I walked across the parking lot, heading to a spot where I knew the cameras lacked sufficient coverage, but still cautiously looking over my shoulder for anyone who might be watching me. Coming to my rental, I wiped away any potential fingerprints of mine then slashed both tires on the driver's side of the brand new Chevy Cruze.

I had three phones now. Two were mine, but one was a gift from the mystery man in Chicago. Wanted to chuck that one in the bay, but decided the trouble he could cause might not be worth it. For now, I stowed it back in my pocket, knowing I would have to turn it on at a predetermined time. On one of the others, I called Hertz.

"This is Russell Dillon," I said when the operator answered. "I rented one of your cars and now somebody's slashed the tires." Acting irate and frustrated, I provided the operator with the hotel information and location of the car then went inside where I left the keys with the front desk.

By the time they would arrive, I would be long gone.

And neither Hertz nor Cathy would ever hear of a Russell Dillon again.

10

It took a little over an hour to get from Emeryville to Stockton in the "borrowed" Honda with bad headlights. I exited the West Side Freeway, coming to a cheap apartment complex on West Benjamin Holt Drive where Sophia still maintained a place there under one of her aliases. My eyes in the area confirmed she was here as recently as last month. And she wasn't alone. But as someone who changed shoes like one would a stick of gum, I never took her for sentimental. Especially for a place far below her current financial means.

I stared out into the predawn night. Looked at the units, barren of any signs of activity this early, while trying to talk myself out of this stupid course of action. Nothing needed to be said since Miami. But maybe she was responsible for the mysterious CIA agent having a hard-on for me. Questions. That's it. A good justification for wanting to see her face-to-face. And since I was in NoCal, no time like the present. I took a handkerchief and wiped down the steering wheel, gearshift, and radio knob before getting out and walking across the crowded parking lot.

Last time I'd come here, I broke in.

Intent on killing her as an act of revenge.

Instead, I'd left enlightened about the woman I loved.

A woman who wasn't Sophia, but who she'd worked with to betray me.

This time, I knocked like a gentleman. Didn't expect anyone to answer on the first—nor any—knock this time of morning. But I did it again, intensely fearing a bullet coming through the door. Instead, the door lock turned after an eye peered through the peephole.

"Truth!" Sophia blurted out and she rushed to hug me.

"Good morning," I said awkwardly, gradually embracing her. "Sorry I didn't bring donuts."

"Donuts make you fat. But bring some next time anyway . . . the ones with the sprinkles. You smell like champagne and sex," she replied, playfully pushing me in my chest as she shook her head in mock disgust. "Didn't know if you were still alive. You coulda sent up a smoke signal or somthin'. Wanna come inside?"

"Sure. If your company doesn't mind."

"Oh," she muttered, her voice dropping down an octave. She backed away slightly, suddenly concerned about her morning attire—a short little white cotton robe. Old habits with me dissipating while older habits with him reestablishing. Then her normal brashness reasserted itself. "Fuck him. He's still *looking for work* and seeing his P.O. on the regular. I pay the rent around here. Come on in."

Everything was as I remembered.

Sophia's floor no longer bore evidence of my gunshots years before, yet the apartment had an even greater eyesore. The man I'd heard all about, but was finally meeting.

"Who the fuck are you?" the man, a good three inches taller than me, asked as he walked from out of the bedroom wearing nothing but a pair of boxers. Nice of him to at least put them on.

"Babe, this is Truth," Sophia calmly answered for me as I clenched my fists, preparing for whatever. I knew coming here might ignite a shit storm, but didn't let that stop me.

"Oh," he said, suddenly deflating his chest and chiseled abs. Ivan was a pretty boy, just as his file said, but the nasty scar on the edge of his scalp just above his left eye told a tale of the harsh realities of prison life. "That's your real name, man? Like 'truth or dare'?"

Sophia and I shared a look. A private joke Ivan had plodded right into. "Yeah. Just like that," I replied, politely smiling.

"Appreciate your lookin' out for my girl while I was away," he said as he sat on the arm of the couch directly behind Sophia, his hand coming to rest on her thigh. With his other hand, he extended a fist pound.

"Someone had to. Crazy world out there," I replied, wondering how much Sophia had shared about me and what I do.

"Heard she learned all kinds of tricks under you," he said with a gleam in his eye. That answered it. Maybe I should've allowed him to stay in prison. Would've been simple enough to cook up something to extend his stay. But I'd seen no reason for them to be apart any longer. For he was Sophia's burden to bear.

"You might say that. She was a good student. Models are generally good at following instructions," I spat, suddenly irritated with the both of them. Two of the *pretty people* for which the world drops everything to accommodate in most scenarios.

Ivan chuckled. "I . . . I was a model," he mumbled, breathing heavily. Just then I think he became self-conscious of the imperfection gracing his forehead.

"I know," I said smartly. "And didn't you do time for beating a woman?"

Sophia's mouth fell open, any hint of a sleepy daze burning away.

"You got jokes. It was a man and a woman. Bitch was fucking up game I was runnin' on a friend o' hers. *And that nigga?* He just got in the way," Ivan said, happy with his justification as he shifted on the sofa's arm. "Ask Sophia. She knows," he further offered.

I turned to look at his less-than-proud coconspirator. But she averted her eyes. Didn't matter. Had accessed and read both their criminal files, frontward and backward courtesy of a friend of mine with California probation and parole. What Ivan wasn't going to share was that the woman wound up turning the tables on him and beating his ass. I allowed him to keep his manhood.

"Besides, I wasn't myself then," the idiot stated, mouth still going. "Was on some shit in a bad way. Clean now."

"Uh huh," I replied succinctly.

"Don't try actin' all high and mighty, nigga. If you been around my girl, then you ain't no saint either. Is there some other reason you're showing up unannounced and comin' at me like this?" he asked as he stood up, moving Sophia aside.

"Nope. Just shit and giggles. I'm really a stand-up comedian. And weak-ass dudes who hit women are a good source of material."

Ivan got in my face, puffing up.

"Stop! This ain't no dick measuring contest, y'all two," Sophia finally interjected as she wedged her body between us. "Ivan, yeah, I fucked him a time or two while you were away. But that shit's over. I'm here with you now, ain't I? You happy?" she said as she wrapped her arms around him and rested her head against his chest. Breathing heavily, he backpedaled but continued to glare at me. "And, Truth. Stop fucking with people. Ivan ain't did shit to you," she added for me.

I nodded apologetically to her. Since it was her place.

"So what you want?" Ivan asked.

"Just a spot to clean up and lay my head for a few hours. Then I'll be on my way. Nothing else," I said, holding my open hands outstretched. He didn't really know me, so Sophia's eye roll went unnoticed.

"Well . . . make yourself at home then. Me and my girl goin' back to sleep. Be up in a little bit. C'mon, babe," he said, taking his girlfriend along back to the bedroom. Sat briefly on the couch. Long enough to see Sophia's robe fall off, a sliver of white dropping to the floor. Exposing her bare, sensual backside just as the door slammed shut. Before it could fully register, the bedroom door abruptly opened again. To my surprise, it was Ivan, except he didn't want anything. Had dropped his drawers, giving me an unwanted image as he turned and skulked away to join Sophia in the bed. Motherfucker just wanted me to see and hear it all.

Rather than just storming off like the bitch he wanted me to be, I played the contrarian. Sat there and took my medicine while a man I instantly despised fucked a woman for which I somewhat cared like it was his dying act. Saw her legs split wide to welcome him in an impressive display of flexibility. Heard his grunts as he pounded away between those very legs like a mad bull.

Heard the mattress yielding as she gasped, orgasms convincing me of the pleasure she was experiencing as her hands crept up and down his back.

First job for which I'd hired Sophia was blackmail. Vegas.

Had watched her fucking then.

But through a hidden camera. No audio.

And with a woman.

Then I was aroused. Turned on like a motherfucker. Here, it bordered between displeasure and envy.

For what felt like an eternity later, when she rolled atop Ivan, talking dirty as she cursed him in the myriad ways that drive a man crazy, I'd reached my limits. As I got off the couch, she looked over her shoulder from out the dark.

I imagined her smiling and smiled back. A grin that said, "The two of you win."

The shower eliminated all traces of my drunken romp with Cathy back in Emeryville. Helped sober me up too. I turned the shower nozzle to the off position, noticing all noise had diminished in the apartment. No thumping, creaking, or moaning. Just the sound of water swirling slowly down the bathtub drain. As I pushed aside the shower curtain and stepped out, I was startled by Sophia.

"Privacy's not a priority around here, I see," I said dryly. Her hair was a mess, but the rest of her commanded my attention. I wondered what was on her always devious mind.

"Did you have to bring up his past?" she asked, not bothering to hand me a towel.

"I needed to know if all that's in his past. Kinda like a big brother would do. Yeah," I responded, smiling. "And aren't you worried he's going to catch you in here?"

"Nah. Not after all this *good-good* I put on him. He'll be asleep until noon," she answered with a bit of casual pride to her tone. "What do you really want, Truth?"

"Was in area. For real," I said as I reached past her, she now the one smelling of spent passion, grabbing the towel off the rack. "Wanted to check on you. And to see your boy face-to-face. You could do so much better."

"Like who? You?" she asked, grabbing my dick and squeezing. I grimaced in pain before she let go. "You rejected me, remember?"

"And you got me shot, remember?" I countered, motioning at the physical reminder. Knew it hurt her to look at it. "Wasn't in an affectionate mood at that moment. Does he know about your financial state?"

"No. Ivan might be my boo, but I don't trust him like that. He keeps hounding me about taking a job . . . like the kinds me and you used to do."

"So, you've really been here in this dump the entire time? Playing broke? Looks like you traded one prison for another."

She said nothing. Allowed me to finish drying myself off while standing idly by in the intimate confines we were sharing. Wasn't like her to let that jab go without a counter. Then something struck me.

"Or is what you took from the prince still too hot to touch?" I queried as I squinted at her.

"Being extra cautious. S'all."

"You sure?"

"Yes," she asserted. "Why?"

"Got pulled off my flight on the way here," I spouted, finally getting to the nagging question to which I needed to see her reaction face-to-face. "Government. Heavy shit. Knew about me. Know anything about?"

"No. Why would I?"

"That same shit down in Florida with your prince. They mentioned it. Have photos of us too from when I sprung you. Now I'm on somebody's radar. And I don't like it. Not how I operate. Last time I was flying this blind, you were the one helping to set me up," I said gruffly as I pulled up my pants.

"Was waiting for that," Sophia said with a chuckle. "It always comes back to Collette. The woman wanted you dead and you still carry the torch for her. If you could've heard the way she talked about you when she first hired me . . ."

"I deserved her hatred. I killed her husband."

"Not directly. Unintended consequences. You said so yourself. Remember? Then in the end, you let her think she'd killed you just to give her some fuckin' closure. And if she knew you were alive now, she'd still want you dead. So why can't you forgive me? It was a job, Truth. That's all."

"I forgave you long ago. It's the current shit that has me pissed off."

"So . . . what do these people want?" Sophia asked, appearing spooked.

"A job. They want me to do a job."

"And?"

"I dunno. Not yet at least," I replied, glaring at her. "But I will."

"And?" she asked again. This time a little more smartly as she folded her arms. I waited 'til I pulled my shirt down over my head.

"Expecting a call on a certain day at a certain time. That's all I have to go on for the moment. And if I find out you're holding out again on something I need to know, I'm not going to let our history temper what I do."

"Fuck you, Truth. Fuck you and your threats," she spat as she flung the bathroom door open and stepped aside. The steam from the shower was met by the cooler air of the hallway. "Go. Leave. Just get out, you paranoid asshole."

"Looks like it's your turn for that shower," I said as I walked up to her and sniffed along her neck. "Your tub drains slowly by the way," I said just as I kissed her on the lips and took my leave.

It would be daylight in about an hour.

And sometime after that when she'd notice her car was missing.

On my way out, I lifted her keys from her bedroom while she remained in the bathroom. Right out from under the nose of a slumbering and snoring Ivan.

Yeah. Her *good-good* was that good.

11

Way Back . . .

"See, Mommy told you it was okay," she said as she led me by the hand past all kinds of lights and machines. We were at her job . . . a TV studio. Except it wasn't hers. Not anymore anyways.

My mom was on the soap opera *The Edge of Nowhere,* where she had played "Lettie Hunter from the wrong side of the tracks" . . . Whatever that was. At least until they told her not to come back no more. It was after she'd had her heart broken by Trent Massey. But it wasn't make-believe like on her show because he played Randall Fischer on *Promises for Tomorrow,* a show where he did all kinds of good stuff with other pretty ladies. But none of them were as pretty as my mom, even when she'd been crying.

"Trent!" she shouted out to him while he was in front of a camera talking to Irene Fuller. I knew her from *Promises for Tomorrow* too. She got married a lot, but maybe she'd say hi to me and my mom too. Randall Fischer had told my mom in front of me that he didn't want anything more to do with her, but maybe he was acting then. Just like he was now with Irene Fuller.

Someone yelled, "Cut!" and I heard people complaining about my mom. But not Randall Fischer. He saw her and walked somewhere else. My mom began yelling.

Saying bad things first then begging next. She'd been like this for weeks, but now was worse.

"Ms. Marie," they called out to her when they saw who it was. That's how the TV people called her . . . Leila Marie. No last name. Just her first and middle. She never gave me a middle. Just my first—Truth. After the place in New Mexico where I was born, Truth or Consequences. Anyway, two men came toward her and she ran away, pulling me by the arm behind her, as she tried to get closer to the room that Randall Fischer had gone into. She was scaring me.

"Mommy, can we go?" I asked.

"Trent! I demand that you come over here and speak to me! I'm not leaving until you do!" she yelled, ignoring me. When more people tried to stop her, she tossed a fruit tray from off the table at them. They ducked and most of the cantaloupe and grapes missed. I was already hungry and my stomach growled over the wasted food all over the floor. Wanted to grab just a piece. Then she threw a pitcher filled with somebody's orange juice. That didn't miss.

We were going to be in so much trouble.

A man in a uniform grabbed my mom in a bear hug once he cornered us. She screamed and kicked while he carried her away from the set with another shoving me along behind them. The one carrying my mom kicked the door open to the real world outside. I squinted from all the light that was coming in. People wearing all kinds of clothes and costumes pointed and laughed at us as they walked by to other little buildings with signs on them. Other Randall Fischers and people from the wrong side of the tracks playing make-believe I guessed.

The man who was in charge came outside and tried to get my mom to calm down.

"Leila," he said as he had the man in the uniform put her down. "You can't come around here like this. You know better."

I could tell he felt sorry for her and it calmed her down even though she still wanted to see Randall Fischer. Except he told her Randall didn't want to see her. Ever. Not play acting. This man knew my mom from *The Edge of Nowhere* where he worked before. He reached in his pocket and gave her some money. More money that I had ever seen. Told her to leave. And to get some help.

She told him that the Trent man was the only one who could help her. He was about to say something else then he saw me standing there. The man who pushed me outside was still behind me, so I was afraid to move.

"Leila, you never told us you had a son. And Trent sure as hell didn't," he said to my mom.

"That's because he's been away in boarding school. Until I was fired," she answered him, lying. Or maybe she was just play acting. I'd never been at a boarding school. Had never attended school. Just a steady diet of old books and the TV in the awful, scary hotel where we stayed.

"Why you didn't tell them about me, Mommy?" I asked on the bus ride away from the studio. I remembered the night when she brought Randall Fischer by our hotel. When he first found out about me and where we lived, that's when he broke up with her. And when she changed.

"Because you're Mommy's secret," she said as she counted the money the nice man had given her. "And if people don't know about you, they can't hurt you, baby. No one can ever hurt you."

"Oh. So . . . where are we going now? Back to New Mexico?" I asked with a smile, hoping that was the answer. I had friends back there. Here in Hollywood, I never spoke to anyone. Just the TV and my mom . . . when she'd come back from work. Sometimes she'd stay gone long. But I kept the door locked just like I promised.

"I wanted to go to Seattle. Trent was from there originally. Heard it was so pretty," she said with a sigh as she stopped counting the money. "But that doesn't matter anymore."

The city bus took us to a Greyhound bus station filled with lots of people going places. We got out and my mom went to a pay phone where she made a call. She seemed even sadder as she spoke too low for me to hear. When she was done, she bent down to talk to me.

"We're going see your Uncle Jason. In New Orleans," she said.

"Is it somewhere nice? And happy? Like Disneyland?" I asked, hoping it was.

"New Orleans has its own magic, Truth," she answered, forcing a smile for me I think.

Then she took me by the hand to buy our tickets out of Hollywood.

12

Seattle

I jogged along Alki Beach; the cloud-shrouded Olympic Mountain range barely visible across Puget Sound from me. Felt safe here. Relatively. If I needed to flee the country on short notice, Canada was just a prepaid boat ride and bribed border official away. At my one o'clock position was Vashon Island, a ferry in the distance bringing residents from the mainland on schedule. Public transportation was an interesting part of life around here. Boats, bicycles, buses, and trains shuttling bodies to and from the many hills, hamlets, and islands that comprised the area. Of course, city still had its traffic jams; a gift—kind of like gang activity and overpriced home prices—the locals liked to blame on the influx of Californians year in and year out. The good ol' *Seattle Freeze* in effect for outsiders. Of course, that kept people mostly to themselves and out of my business.

Perfect.

With the cooler temperatures and lower humidity, I was just now breaking a sweat as I slowed from full-on sprint to brisk walk. My destination was ahead, a condo on the water's edge I was renting on Beach Drive. I lowered the volume on the Tinie Tempah album to which I'd been listening, enough to hear my labored breathing. I was welcoming the fresh, salty air in my lungs as a middle-aged woman and her barking German shepherd driving by in a Toyota Prius honked. Didn't have enough fingers to count all the fuckin' hybrids in West Seattle. Keeping with the area, I courteously smiled and waved, the woman no doubt trying to figure out if she'd seen the ever-elusive *magical jogging African American* in these here parts before.

Or if he was single.

Inside my place, I disabled the alarm and did a quick once-over to make sure I hadn't any unwanted visitors. The condo was Spartan-like and contemporary, just as I preferred. I'd learned, back in Dallas when I got caught up with the delusion of normalcy, about the perils of being too settled in. Couldn't buy into the illusion no matter how right it felt.

After a quick shower and change of clothes, I turned on the TV. A little background noise while I turned my attention to something else. In the kitchen, I reached into the microwave, which I rarely used. Inside, I'd stowed a small item wrapped in aluminum foil to the back, but now set it down on the kitchen counter. Pulling out a drawer, I grabbed a tiny screwdriver and a pair of disposable latex gloves which I donned.

I carefully peeled back the foil used for jamming signals, still afraid the object might explode via remote. Then, leaving it turned off, I dissected the flip cell phone that was given to me back in Chicago. Wanted to make sure there wasn't anything capable of being tracked even with it turned off. Had repeated this procedure three times since leaving California, each time finding nothing but the obvious phone components.

Had two more days before the call that was to come. And trying to anticipate what the job might be for which I was needed was giving me a headache. Frustrated, I carefully reassembled the phone. Maybe a day down at Pike Place or some idle time at Point Defiance Zoo would be nice for a change. But first, I was craving some fresh hummus and pita bread from Ephesus up on California Avenue.

A harsh knock came on the glass patio window out by the barbecue pit I never used. I hurriedly wrapped up the phone back in the aluminum foil and placed it inside the kitchen drawer along with the gloves and screwdriver. Outside was a girl olive in complexion with dark, full eyebrows and a short pixie cut peering through a pair of cupped hands. Neither intruder nor threat, she was just my neighbor.

I came over, unlocking the door to let her in.

"I'm keeping your dog," the girl said without so much as a greeting, flicking a cigarette back over her shoulder with no regard for my front patio or the beach below. The remaining smoke shot from out her nostrils as she glared at me like I'd done something wrong. But that was just her way. If she were truly mad, I wouldn't be seeing her. Her name was Helene. Or at least that's what she called herself. Upon first warming up to me, she'd told me her parents were professors at the University of Washington. She was still "finding herself," so wasn't suited for academia despite her smarts, which she hid behind an exterior of faux rudeness.

"Guess I can't really object. After all this time, I'm sure he's bonded with you more than me," I said as I allowed her to walk freely inside my space. Same pattern she'd repeat every few months or so when I was in town. Could almost plot every step. Still, hoped she'd stay away from the kitchen this time and my little project. The dog she'd claimed was actually a stray I'd picked up as part of my persona when I first rented here. Helene fell in love with him, sensing a kinship no doubt.

"Damn straight. Me and mutt got a connection," Helene said as she leaned over to look through my telescope set with a clear view of the sound and the southern tip of Bainbridge Island. "Ever caught anybody fucking with this?" she asked as she pulled away from the eyepiece. Was admiring her shape at the moment. She was barefoot, having run over from next door, with shorts not really hiding much of her full hips and ass. On the back of her T-shirt were dates and locales from the rapper Penny Antnee's recent Change Don't Come Easy tour including his stop at KeyArena. Found it funny for reasons I wouldn't be sharing with her.

"Wouldn't tell if I did," I answered smartly as she looked back at me. Her features, a blend of her mixed heritage—Greek from her mom and local Duwamish tribe from her dad—gave her an unusual quality that was not unattractive. Of course, she played that down.

"When did you get back?" she asked as she finally warmed up enough to give me a hug. As they embraced me, I had no idea what the tats covering both her inner forearms represented. In addition to the cigarette smoke in her hair, I also detected the smell of apples.

"Late last night. Buster doing okay?" I asked about the mutt, changing the subject from my arrival time.

"Yeah. Except I changed his name. It's Marshawn now."

"Like Marshawn Lynch? The football player?" I asked.

"No. After an ex of mine. He was a dog too. Are you a dog, Brandon? Don't be a dog," she spat machinegun-like without so much as a breath between words.

"So where's 'Marshawn' now?" I asked, honestly interested in seeing him after all these months.

"At Seward Park with my older sister. She and her family have a collie and they let them chase the ducks together. Where did you go this time?" she quizzed as she dropped across my sofa.

"All over," I replied, knowing she hated my nonchalance, but welcomed the challenge of drawing more out of me. I plopped down beside her, letting her reposition her legs so they rested across my lap. It was a game with us. A little more revealed each time. Or so she thought.

"For a photographer, I never see your work. Not even in your own place," she remarked at the bare walls as I rested my hand on her bare knee. To her my name was Brandon. Claimed to have grown up in the Pacific Northwest back when my dad was stationed at Fort Lewis and simply reconnecting with the past. The jet-setting photographer angle provided an excuse for my infrequent stays.

"I don't like to show off. Besides, don't need anyone breaking in while I'm gone. I keep most of my stuff at the studio. Got a little place by the Amazon offices on South Lake Union," I said, weaving a bit of fiction that I felt sounded believable.

"Little place? By Amazon? Yeah. Explains why you're renting here. Probably can afford one of those mansions on Mercer Island, but feel it would make you look too pretentious," Helene joked as she stretched. Felt those powerful legs as they tensed then released, her toes wiggling at the end.

"That's the story you've written for me. Guess I'll stick with it," I stated, smiling. "How do you afford your place? Plasma donations at the blood bank?"

"Cute. Parents. My mom says I'm too irrepressible to stay under her roof, so I get my solitude and freedom on these desolate shores. You should meet them sometime."

"Why? We're getting married or something?" I joked.

"Depends. If you treat me right, maybe we can play house," Helene said, teasing her short, dark hair. An awkward hush fell over us. "Can you treat me right, Brandon?" she asked, no longer just fucking with me. Now it was about fucking me.

I wasn't sure what I was about to say . . . or do, but a buzzing sound interrupted us. Both of us looked around before I realized it was my personal phone. Had left it next to the TV.

"Um . . . I need to get that," I uttered. Ass could wait. Especially ass that might complicate things for me. I was up here to avoid complications. Still, I'd be lying if I said I wasn't down for a good fuck.

Helene pouted, biting her bottom lip rather than saying whatever had popped into her head. Then she relented, moving her legs aside in a slow, deliberate, sweeping arc. Gave me a chance to reconsider whether that call was really that important. I deliberated, letting my fingers linger as her knee slid out from under them, then got up.

On my phone, I had a single text message:

Where the fuck is my car, nigga? I know u took it. Will cut off ur balls . . . after I fuck u.

I chuckled, realizing it was from Sophia. Had left her car safely in Vancouver, just across the border from Oregon. But before I could respond, Helene grabbed my phone away from me.

"Let's see what . . . or who has you smiling like that," she said, backing away from my outstretched hand. At first she giggled, her eyes going between my phone and me. Then her brow furrowed.

"What?" I asked, still smiling. Message was harmless enough.

"Oh my God," she said as she slowly handed my phone back to me. "I didn't realize you were . . ."

I waited for her to complete whatever her thought was. *Seeing someone? Involved? A ho?*

"Gay," she said as she completed her thought.

Gay? That wasn't one of the phrases I'd guessed. What the fuck?

Then as I brought my eyes back to the phone, I figured it out. Of course, for safety and security, I didn't have the number stored under Sophia's name. It was under Albert, a dude's name.

"I feel so, so foolish," Helene said, covering her mouth before I could clear things up. Looked as if she wanted to go crawl under a rock and never ever see the light of day again. "The little dog. The industry you're in. Hell, even this place. I shoulda known," she grunted, throwing her hands up.

"It . . . it's okay. I wanted to tell you, but didn't know how to," I lied, feeling the last traces of my hard-on fading away. Wouldn't be getting any ass from her now, but also wouldn't be having her pry much either.

Concessions.

"Um . . . I need to go. Yeah," my friend and neighbor mumbled to herself as she shuffled by. Dazed and dejected.

And then I was left alone.

Helene promised she'd return, but . . .

She felt she'd made a fool of herself. And I let her live with that feeling.

I walked over to my telescope. Repositioned it for something a lot closer.

Watched Helene as she walked along the beach . . . alone.

I'd never used the telescope to watch someone fucking.

Only to watch someone I'd fucked with.

13

My phone rang.

Right on the day he said he'd call. And at the time he said he'd call.

This was really going down.

"Hello," I answered, seeing the call was coming from a blocked number.

"You didn't throw away the phone. Smart man."

"Want to tell me what you want?"

"Not over the phone. Take down this address. I won't repeat it either."

I listened, writing down the information he provided on a scrap of paper. When he was finished, I had a question.

"This isn't right around the corner for me. How do you expect me to get there on short notice? I might be out of the country," I said, continuing to walk briskly past people, the phone pressed against my ear so as to better hear.

"But you're not," he replied. "Because I told you not to leave the country when I gave you that phone. And because you're currently in Portland, Oregon. Heading east on Couch Street. Toward the river. How is Old Town? I can hear all the people in the background, too, by the way."

I stopped on the dime, saying nothing as I surveyed my surroundings. Felt my stomach knot up as I carefully backed away from everyone around me. Didn't stop until I was free of the crowd and next to a stairwell. Ready to flee if this didn't go as planned.

"Now that we understand each other, see that you make it. On time," he said with a smirk that I could see through the phone.

After he hung up, I waited a while longer. Allowed myself a smirk of my own. Then I used my phone with which I'd just spoken to him.

My phone.

Not the one he thought he was speaking to me on. That phone was somewhere else.

Dialed a number to someone.

"You okay?" I asked the person who was in Portland instead of me. And apparently heading east on Couch Street. In a nasal tone, he answered that he was.

"Good," I said. "They're tracking the phone's GPS. Turn it off again and dump the battery. And get out of there."

If someone was physically in Portland, they wouldn't catch him. The teenager was Wally Dunwoody, a student at Portland Community College, but also a parkour legend in Oregon. Could leap, jump, and flip like a spider monkey based on the YouTube clips I'd seen of him. Adrenaline junkie that he was, it only took a grand and the possibility of danger to get him to take the phone and turn it on at the right time. I'd already set all calls to be forwarded from it to my phone.

Satisfied so far, I dialed another number.

"Did you get it?" I asked cryptically of the man who answered.

"Working on it. Gotta do discreetly," the man I had monitoring cell phone tower transmissions around the Old Town area of Portland replied in a low tone, in case his coworkers were being nosy. Money wasn't the answer for everyone. For him, it was that long elusive acceptance letter from Stanford that would be coming for his daughter.

"Just get something for me as soon as you can," I said from behind sunglasses and a Mariners baseball cap. Then I ended the call.

Sloppy of whomever he was to think I'd follow his instructions without a few ideas of my own.

And for him to not figure it out.

Told me a lot about him and his current state.

He was far from infallible . . . and desperate.

Left Pike Place Market whistling to myself.

For I had somewhere to be per my instructions.

14

Oklahoma City

I was in the main bar of Mickey Mantle's Steakhouse. Manning a booth seat against the memorabilia-laden wall while I enjoyed a meal of pepper steak with fresh broccoli and mushroom risotto. Took a look at the time on my phone while I drank from my glass of water.

Was in the right city.

Right time.

Wrong location.

Just trying to put things back on my terms.

My instructions were to meet with the mystery man by the water taxi on the canal here in Bricktown. But I wanted a good steak, so I sent some poor schmuck to summon him to me instead. Told my messenger to look for a pompous, gangly asshole who looked like he was used to giving orders.

Dressed differently than when he first met me, I motioned him over when he entered the restaurant. Seeing the pissed look on his face brought joy to my soul. While I wore a sun visor, T-shirt, and cargo shorts, he was in jeans and a button down with Ray-Bans shielding his eyes. Had a folded newspaper under his arm that I hoped didn't contain a gun.

Something unusual happened as he approached. The pictures on two of the TVs above the bar developed static when he walked by. Then a guy who'd come from the ballpark across the street began experiencing problems with his phone, even losing a call, when he passed as well. My guest had some sort of jamming device on him. Afraid of being recorded or my having a wire on me.

And I thought I was the paranoid one.

"You don't follow instructions very well," he said as he sat down opposite me. From behind the false smile, he kept his voice to a barely audible murmur.

"Was hungry," I retorted. "So what should I call you?"

"Mr. Smith," he replied, dead serious.

"Let me guess. First name John, huh?" I joked as I continue to eat. Annoyed the fuck out of him. "You got me here. What's the job?"

He looked around at the full bar.

"They're not paying attention. Relax. It's OKC. Ignoring the McVeigh bombing, how much clandestine shit happens here?"

"You'd be surprised," he offered.

"Want something to drink? You must be thirsty waiting around by the canal for me. Have some water," I suggested, motioning to the extra glass of water before him. Our eyes met.

"You take me for a fool?" he asked, avoiding touching it. Wasn't going to leave a fingerprint for me.

"Speaking of being a fool, whatever this job is, I'm not a hero. And despite what it looked like from behind your little spy cameras, that job down in Florida wasn't on that level. For real. I don't fuck with terrorists, so don't expect me to suddenly become patriotic. Don't operate like that."

"Relax. It's something more intimate. Discrete. Admire the way you were able to get inside Prince Abdel Al-Bin Sada's compound and get out with your life. And with the body count of trained pros you've racked up, it's the perfect balance of stealth and ruthlessness." He unfolded the newspaper and slid a single photo into view. This time, it wasn't of me. "I need this man reassigned to another position," he said. Dude was used to ordering the *reassignment* of people.

"I'm no hit man. Don't rock like that. Get someone else."

"Still proclaiming your innocence. I know what I've seen with my own two eyes," Mr. Smith pushed back. "Now . . . if he is accidentally reassigned like the rest of the unlucky people in your life, or even if you want somebody else to get their hands dirty, you'll get the job done."

A woman who'd entered walked by. Tall, blond, and confident in a black party dress. Most conversations in the restaurant, including ours, ceased. Should've had her own theme music. As she strolled down the side of the bar nearest us, one of the bar patrons was a little overzealous. In trying to discretely get her attention, he accidentally bumped into her arm. The black clutch she carried in her hand popped free, falling forward next to our booth.

"I got it, miss," Mr. Smith said as he leaned down, snatching up her clutch in a smooth manner I wouldn't have expected from him. I guess we were both used to wearing different faces depending on the scenario.

"Thank you so much, sir," she said as Mr. Smith returned the clutch to her. She smiled at both of us before joining her companions who were seated in the leather chairs along the back wall.

"Who is he?" I asked, removing my hand from over the photo as we got back down to business.

"DA," he answered, his eyes still lustfully on the woman who made a favorable impression. "Down in Orleans Parish."

"In Louisiana? New Orleans?" I asked, my eyes narrowing as I looked at the photo again. He didn't know who I really was, so a job in New Orleans was a coincidence. Still, it was as if the fates were conspiring against me. Apt, I suppose. "I already told you I don't kill. Now I know you definitely have the wrong guy. No law enforcement and definitely no district attorney."

"This isn't a negotiation. And your continued freedom of movement is your payment."

"Fuck you. I know this isn't sanctioned by your people. Do it yourself."

"Can't," he replied. "Too busy keeping the world safe."

"Why do you want him gone?" I asked.

"You don't get that kind of info. Protects you. Protects me. Just know that I need it done," Mr. Smith replied.

"You're here alone. I'm pretty sure of that. If I were what you think me to be, what's to stop me from—"

He cut me off. "Know why I picked this city for our meeting?" he casually asked as he turned to see what was playing on the TVs in the bar for the first time. It was as if he'd been saving this moment for last. Free to relax.

"Of course. For the steaks," I said as I plopped the final piece of steak in my mouth. "Right? Or are you hoping to see Kevin Durant?"

He kept his eyes locked on *SportsCenter*. Barely acknowledging me or my taunts. "Because it's close to

Dallas . . . where I just left. You are familiar with Dallas, yes?"

Collette.

He was threatening me with Collette.

15

Dallas

Bob Jones Park in Southlake.

Had sped the 200 miles down I-35 to get here, lucky not to get a ticket. Had to be sure Collette was okay, but couldn't shake the raw feelings stirred from our last encounter years ago. Our final encounter.

Right here.

She'd held a gun on me that night. One I'd provided.

"Is that why you lied to the police? Wanted to kill me yourself? That is what you want to do, right? That's why I brought the gun for you. I lied to you. Betrayed you. Now you can finish it," I'd said.

"And . . . you . . . deserve . . . to . . . die, you bastard!" Collette had said, baring her teeth as she bordered on hyperventilating. "You took away the one person in the world who meant something to me!"

"I'm sorry for that, Collette," I'd said, pained as I came to realize that despite the momentary fantasy of the past few months, I never had a chance. As angered as I'd been up to that point, the fact that she wanted me dead no longer mattered.

"No, you're not. Don't ever say that!" I heard the hammer click back as Collette prepared to exact her revenge.

"How'd you know? At least tell me that."

"Your voice. I'll never forget your voice. It's like a bell ringing in my head every time you speak. You were there when it happened. You were there when Myron blew himself up. You knew. You . . . killed . . . my husband!"

"He did it to himself, Collette. He was cheating on you. I . . . didn't know he'd—"

"Blow himself up and try to kill me too? What kind of monster are you?"

"One that loves you no matter what you think of me."

"Love? Is that what made you fuck Sophia? Love for me?" Collette shot at my feet, clearly coming to terms with what she was going to do. "It sickened me to do the things I did with you. Don't you dare talk to me about love!"

Collette was blind for a time. Indirectly my fault. Her husband's mistress had hired me to break up his marriage so she could have him all to herself. I went too far. Led him to believe Collette had been cheating on him. And he blew himself up. Gas explosion that took out the whole house. Just as Collette was coming in the door.

It was one of my first jobs as a free agent. No longer under the direction of Jason North, a devil who used me as his personal tool in many of his schemes of blackmail, coercion, and revenge. Mutual interests later led Jason to sell me out to Collette, revealing the truth about the man she'd accepted into her life. A man she knew as Chris the author.

And she went after it with a passion; convincing me she was still blind as her eyes got better and hiring Sophia as part of her plan for vengeance.

Worst of all, she allowed me to fall in love with her.

Funny thing was, in the end Collette couldn't bring herself to shoot me. Took someone else to pull the trigger.

That person who was arriving just now, Frisco Police emblazoned on the side of his patrol car. Elicited a different set of emotions from me as I wasn't wearing a bulletproof vest this time.

I'd called him when I crossed the Texas state line. Told him I needed to meet with him urgently. Seeing as he was still on duty, he'd sped here on Texas State Highway 121 no doubt. Last time we were here, he was Dallas PD. Officer Kane was Collette's protector back then. And a man who helped me give the woman I loved closure.

Now?

He was so much more.

I exited my rental car and motioned toward him. Officer Kane exited as well, but left his car running with the window down. We were alone in this wooded area, but he turned his head several times, surveying the tree line with one hand resting atop his holster as he dipped his dark sunglasses with the other.

"Relax. I came alone," I said as I carefully strode toward him in the loose gravel.

When I got within ten feet, he suddenly reacted. Drew his gun on me. "I told you what I'd do if I ever saw your ass again!" he yelled, all too well reminding me. "Now get your hands up!"

"I know," I said, complying as Kane closed the distance between us. "But I—"

Didn't finish as the motherfucker cold-cocked me, metal hitting flush against my skull. I tumbled to the ground dazed, but still with enough wits about me to sweep my leg around. Kane wasn't expecting it and fell hard as his feet went out from under him, joining me in the dirt. We lunged at one another, colliding with my angling his gun away from me. His sunglasses fell off, leaving him momentarily blinded by the sun when I rolled him onto his back. I head-butted him right in his nose then, making him drop his gun.

I took a hold of it then, jamming it under his chin. "Stop!" I yelled, staring crazily into his eyes. Didn't have time for this shit. When Kane finally relaxed, I got off him and helped him to his feet.

"You got that out your system?" I asked, covered in dust and scratches as I felt the welt forming on my forehead. He nodded, holding his bloody nose as he looked at his gun still being pointed at him. I applied the safety then tossed it back to him underhanded.

"What the fuck you want?" he asked; breathing heavily as he slowly restored his sidearm to its holster.

"Collette," I replied. "Is she okay?"

"Of course. You're the only one that brings trouble to her life."

"Then I apologize in advance. But there might be some problems."

"What now? Can't you just . . . die or something? I'm serious. Just trying to have a quiet life with my—"

"Wife," I said, completing it for him although it pained me to do so. "I see the wedding band. Am I right? Congratulations. And I see you switched jobs, too. Moving on up to the north side, huh? "

"Yeah," he said, a bit of honest pride showing on his face. "Got a promotion. Things looking up."

"I'm happy for y'all. For real. Glad she's put all the 'stuff' behind her."

"I didn't say all that. Still hard sometimes. But she's made a lot of progress."

"I understand," I responded, taking some solace that maybe a tiny part of Collette missed me. Wouldn't admit that to Kane though. "Well . . . I came to warn you. Somebody knows about her and her connection to me. Somebody that's using it as leverage to get me to do a job."

"Are you saying they're threatening Collette?"

"Yeah. I owe you that much to let you know."

"Must be legit for you to be worried. Well, if anyone comes around, they'll run into more than they planned for."

"You don't understand. This guy is way above your pay grade. Works in the government."

"Our government?" he asked, smiling as if he didn't believe me. Then the smile disappeared.

"Yeah. The dirty stuff if I had to guess. Has a lot of authority. The kind to stop airplanes 'n' shit. As long as I do this, it's all good. But . . ." I said, feeling uncomfortable sharing my doubts with him.

"So, what are you going to do?" he asked.

"I'm going to do the damn job," I replied. "Just wanted to let you know. Keep an eye out for your wife. Just in case."

"You think I won't?"

"No. I'm just saying if you need some additional security . . . discrete security, I can put a few extra eyes on Collette. Figured I'd come to you first."

"Fuck you. You've done enough. Keep your . . . your resources. I'm the fuckin' police and ain't nothin' happenin' to Collette on my watch, so just stay the fuck away."

"Uh huh. King Kong ain't got nuthin' on you, Denzel. Well, fine. Protect and serve," I muttered as I walked off toward my rental. "Just do your job and I'll do mine."

"It's not a job, bitch. I love her," he called out from behind me. Angst was evident in his voice.

"Good. Continue to do so. Because if you ever hurt her, you'll have to answer to me. And unlike today, I won't call first," I said as I got back inside the Hyundai and started it. Not the brightest thing I'd done, threatening a police officer.

As I drove by Kane, he kicked my car door. Hurling expletives, but at least he didn't shoot. Hated to bring my shit in on his and Collette's lives, but couldn't undo it or magically make it go away.

Like a bad case of diarrhea, this had to run its course.

As I exited the park and turned onto Highway 114, en route to DFW Airport after a change of clothes, I made a call.

Despite Kane's wishes, there would be a few extra sets of eyes on Collette besides his buddies on the force.

My wedding gift to them.

16

I flew into Louis Armstrong International Airport posing as a Texas gambler, in town for some high stakes poker at Harrah's and checked into the W Hotel in as visible a way as possible. On a more low-key note, I then checked into the Holiday Inn on Loyola by the Superdome under a completely different alias. This would be my real base of operations as I went about figuring what I was going to do about the unfortunate district attorney.

I was reading NOLA.com online while listening to WWL radio to get back up to speed on the vibe of the city where I grew up.

His name was Rodney Roy, a Creole brother from New Orleans's Seventh Ward who was a good Catholic boy and graduate of St. Augustine High School. Law degree was from Southern University over in Baton Rouge. Had originally clerked in the Civil District Court of Orleans Parish before transitioning over to the criminal side of things and his career in the prosecutor's office. After serving as assistant DA, he'd won overwhelmingly in election to the top spot in the months after Hurricane Katrina on a platform of a no-nonsense approach to dealing with criminals who'd slipped through the "gaping cracks in our system." Cracks he promised to seal shut even if it took his last breath.

Breathe, Rodney. Breathe.

I was munching on a still-warm beignet from Café du Monde when I found an article on Rodney . . . and his family. Shit.

Had a wife and daughter.

Of course he couldn't be a hedonistic, egotistical bachelor.

Had to be a family man.

I took a deep breath and exhaled while the information on the monitor before me set in. On the outside, he seemed like a good person. But I'd learned that people have two sides, sometimes more. What was his relationship with Mr. Smith? Under ordinary circumstances, I would've turned down the job.

Murder.

I was in town to commit murder.

And not being paid for it either.

Despite my being a less-than-admirable person, my aims were to make you wish you were dead. Not straight take you out.

Well . . . not most times.

Not going to lie, hands weren't clean.

Shot and killed two people in my life. Other times, I either missed or they were shooting at me. First one was a rapper. Loup Garou the Haitian Werewolf they called him. Was first lieutenant of rapper, actor, and businessman Penny Antnee, a guy whose secret I'd uncovered. In that instance, Loup Garou had tried bodying me first . . . and failed. Feet still ache when I think back to the New Mexico desert. Also led me to believe he'd murdered Collette, so felt I was her avenging angel when I put a round in his skull.

Other person to die by my hand was Jason North. Despite my being of his blood, that one had it coming.

Maybe more so because I was of his blood. The mythology of the son slaying the father being perpetuated in today's world.

Somebody could justify those, but I was damned from birth, so fuck it. Had to own 'em.

Tired of being cooped up and feeling sorry for myself, I left my hotel room to hit the streets and do some physical reconnaissance.

Being out and about in the 504 brought back many memories. During my time here, On-Phire Records grew from a wannabe to worldwide powerhouse with Jason North as the public face and later totally at the helm. On these very streets, On-Phire was everywhere. As much a part of the scene as Cash Money, No Limit, and Big Boy Records in those days. Release parties, public appearances, concerts, giveaways, and radio appearances from Uptown to Hollygrove; from Mid-City to Tremé; from Gert Town to Gretna; from Ninth Ward to Marrero; from New Orleans East to Gentilly. But below the surface, On-Phire was a heavy-handed organization funded by illegal drug money, promising young up-and-comers the stars while screwing them over with shady contracts and intimidation.

That was my expertise. Finding weaknesses and exploiting them on behalf of Jason North. Through blackmail, shaping the truth or creating our own truth to suit our needs.

God bless America.

So there would be no paper trail, I borrowed a crack rental for a few dollars over off St. Claude Avenue. They wouldn't remember or be able describe me anyway. Drove the musty Ford pickup across the Crescent City Connection over to Algiers where the DA lived in the gated English Turn neighborhood. As I needed to restock some equipment discretely, I stopped at an off-brand computer and electronics store on General DeGaulle Drive for a few pieces.

"My man, I got a list from my boss, but tryin' ta save some money. Ya heard me?" I said through a distinct local mumble as I entered. Rocking baggy jeans, Jordans, and a freshly starched XXL white tee, I handed a handwritten list to the brother behind the counter. Looked familiar, but I'd picked the West Bank for this stop so as to avoid people who might know me.

He scanned items on the list, intentionally written in my worst handwriting. "A lot of surveillance equipment. Is your boss a PI?" he asked.

"Yeah, that's what he call himself," I said, toothpick dangling from my mouth, as I showed him a private investigator's license number that belonged to a firm in Kenner.

"You look familiar. Where you from?" he asked as he rolled his chair over to a computer to check his stock.

"The east," I replied from beneath my fitted New Orleans Saints hat as I peered into the glass showcase, pretending to be interested in the cell phones he also sold. I'd even added fake gold fronts and a water-soluble tattoo of a woman's name on my neck. Pretty memorable if somebody ever had to identify me. "Moved to Texas after Katrina, *mane*. Was in Katy with my auntie 'n' em. Jus' gettin' back now that my money right. You?"

"Out that Nine originally, but been on the West Bank for a minute. Me, my wife Val evacuated with our kids for Katrina. Went up to Atlanta for about three weeks. But we came back. Just some wind damage to the house. Things are still slow even after all these years, but this business is my life. Want to leave a legacy for my kids, y'know. Too many coming up the wrong way. Like I did at first," he admitted as he left his chair and went about gathering the mini cams, cables, wireless nodes, and microphones in an orderly fashion.

"I feel ya," I said as he rang me up. Paid him in cash and motioned to keep the change.

"Thanks, bro. Appreciate your business," he said as he shook my hand. "Lance," he offered.

"Carlos," I responded, with a flash of gold from my mouth.

As I was leaving, I remembered him. Was years ago, but I remembered him. Dude was the straight-laced best friend of one of On-Phire's first true stars, a rapper named AK. Dude was one of Jason's major screw jobs, until he fell to the violence, sending ripples throughout the organization. I was more in the background in those times, but couldn't risk someone else out here finding me vaguely familiar like that Lance dude. Was going to need a sacrificial lamb to finish this job.

Continuing down General DeGaulle, I pulled into a convenience store parking lot across the street from Our Lady of Holy Cross College. Changed my shirt and shoes then affixed magnetic signs to the truck's doors to match the cargo in the bed. Then as I pressed on, I contemplated what this job was really about.

Mr. Smith didn't want Rodney Roy discredited or framed, he wanted him dead. ASAP. Meant it was either something personal or a business issue. Or both. Mr. Smith's desperation was evident in Oklahoma, so he was using me for cleanup. A cleanup he didn't want his bosses to know about. Or connect him to. Was getting somewhere . . . piece by piece.

I crossed the Intracoastal Waterway that brought me by the Orleans-Plaquemines Parish line then took

LA406 over to the English Turn Golf & Country Club. Talked my way past the guardhouse easy enough with a few kind words and some careful name dropping. But when I rolled up to the Roy residence on Island Club Drive, two NOPD patrol cars were parked out front. Security extra tight. Of course, Mr. Smith wouldn't give me an easy job . . . if murder ever could be called easy.

Glad this was just recon, but he wasn't giving me much time before I was made public enemy number one without the Chuck D or Flavor Flav. I drove by and parked the truck on the shoulder, drawing the attention of the NOPD officers closest to me. Gave them a clear view of the borrowed lawn mowers in the back of my crack rental truck as I exited, dripping fresh sweat courtesy of driving without the A/C.

"They don't need no lawn work. Move along," the officer on the passenger said, lowering his window as I approached. No problems with the air conditioning in their car. Had a half-eaten shrimp po-boy resting in his lap. I came closer, ignoring his statement with a big grin.

"Oh. I just finished up some yards ova dere on Pinehurst Drive. That reporter that be on WDSU. Wanted to see if anybody else around here needed anythang before I went home," I offered, shifting to a more disarming accent as I wiped my brow. "My man, what's up? Somebody been shot or somthin'?"

"Nah. You ain't been watchin' the news, bro?" the one behind the wheel chided. "This the DA's house. Keepin' nosey people a safe distance away because of the trial."

"Oooh. Right, right. Wish I had y'all deep like that at my crib. Got a couple old ladies y'all could help me run off," I teased, analyzing the new bit of info about a high-profile trial from behind an amiable grin.

As I carried on with the jokes, the garage door to the DA's house rose. Stole a glance of the garage interior as a white Mercedes GLK emerged. From behind the tint, could make out at least two people inside the SUV as it backed down the driveway toward us.

"I'd love to keep chattin' it up with ya, my man, but all the cold air is getting out and I wanna finish my po-boy," the one closest to me admitted.

"Right, right. You got me wantin' one o' those now. Guess I'll be on my way then," I responded with a nod as I strolled back to my truck.

Despite how good that would be right now, fuck a po-boy.

I had someone to follow.

17

I followed the Benz as it wove its way through Algiers traffic then back across the Crescent City Connection to the East Bank of New Orleans. Had to literally mash the accelerator to the floor just to get the truck up the incline of the bridge and to maintain visual contact. Just in case I lost the SUV, I quickly stored its license plate number and description on my iPhone. On the Pontchartrain Expressway, I closed the distance, staying four cars back as the Benz took the O'Keefe Avenue exit. As we travelled down Howard Avenue, I recognized the Clear Channel Communications building on my left, home to Q93 and WYLD who spun most of New Orleans's hip hop and R&B hits. Music such an important element of the town. Up ahead, my quarry slowed at Lee Circle, the statue of the confederate general still standing watch at its center as he's done since way before my time. I dropped back another car length in case the SUV decided to take the circle all the way around. Instead, a quarter ways around, it made a right turn onto St. Charles Avenue.

As I sped up and merged onto Lee Circle in pursuit, my phone rang in my hand.

"Yes," I answered immediately.

"He just copped something. Took back to the apartment," my eyes back in Stockton, California, said. Still had Sophia's place being watched, but told them to shift their focus to her beau and his comings and goings. Knew that fucker Ivan was still using when I'd met him. He was weak. And not just because he was a former model either.

"Is she home?" I asked. Another white GLK had turned onto St. Charles. Had to be careful I was still tailing the right one, but my attention was split. Between a job I was being forced to do here in New Orleans and a job I'd taken upon myself because . . . sometimes I can be a pure sucker.

"Yeah. She ain't left today," he said.

"She ever been with him when he copped that shit?"

"Uh . . ."

"Talk. Be truthful. Because I'll know if you're lying," I said as I crossed Louisiana Avenue, a Rite Aid pharmacy on my right while the streetcar passed me on the left, en route to the CBD with its human cargo.

"She's scored for him before."

I slapped my hand on the steering wheel just as I struck a pothole. Made the truck swerve badly before I quickly corrected.

"Thinks she's using too?" I asked, clenching the wheel tighter than before.

An unnerving pause filled the airwaves, until he replied, "Can't say . . ."

"All right," I responded sharply.

"Want me to do anything about it?"

"No. Eyes only," I answered. "I'll handle it. Just keep me posted."

Ivan was a full-blown crackhead by the time he went to prison, career and life in shambles. Sophia was his puppy dog then, faithful and devoted to a near fatal fault. Nothing in her records indicated she'd fallen as far as him with the drugs, but . . .

Fuck.

I'd gotten too close.

On both accounts.

The Benz made an abrupt U-turn, doubling back to Nashville Avenue where it made a quick right. Thought it might be trying to shake me, so I continued down St. Charles Avenue and took a left on State Street instead, speeding to intercept it on Magazine Street. Got there in time to stop at the red light in front of Reginelli's Pizzeria just as it crossed directly in front of me. But after it passed, I watched it come to a stop in front of a business on Magazine that shared the structure with Reginelli's.

When my light turned green, I continued straight in the pickup that was now shuddering and sputtering, but quickly turned into the parking lot of WOW Wingery. I drove through, coming around the other side to where I was now facing the place on Magazine Street where the GLK was stopped. Truck was overheating, so this was probably where I was going to abandon it along with the lawn mowers in its bed. I pulled into an open parking spot, going about removing the gold fronts from my teeth and wiping the false tattoo from my neck since I no longer needed the disguise. As I exited, I quickly removed the magnetic landscaping signs off both doors, throwing them in the Wingery's Dumpster along with my discarded clothes. Stowed my electronic surveillance equipment in my backpack and walked away, keeping my baseball hat pulled low.

As I exited onto Magazine Street, I looked up to see where my pursuit had taken me. Across the street, directly in front of me, the pale yellow building read CRESCENT CITY DANCE COMPANY. A thin young girl dressed like a ballerina, who looked to be about fourteen, was exiting the SUV. The driver was a woman, her mom who came around to give her daughter a kiss and to share some words with her. I'd been following the DA's family, but didn't know it until now. From my research, remembered his wife's name was Taralynn and the daughter's name was Sasha. Without staring directly in their direction, I snapped a photo of them with my phone as I walked by, planning on catching a cab somewhere down the block. So I could get back to planning the removal of a husband and father from their lives.

Cold, I know.

As Mrs. Roy pulled away from the dance studio, an old Suburban overtook her then cut her off. Thought it was just a typical New Orleans bad driver in a hurry until it slammed on its brakes, her honking at it alerting me to look back once again.

I'd staged enough set-ups to see the markings of one.

Could've walked away.

Just turn my head and keep on rolling. *I see nothing* like a motherfucker.

But this might be a hit.

And Rodney Roy's wife getting killed might ramp up his security to where I could never get to him.

That's it. Stay cold, Truth. Analytical. Objective.

"Bollocks," I blurted out, figuring American English just didn't do for how annoyed with myself I felt right now. In mid-step, I pivoted around and began heading back toward the scene. The driver remained obscured inside the Suburban as Mrs. Roy steadily honked for it to move, waving his hands as if it had stalled or something. It was too close for her to go around.

Then someone exited out one of the rear doors as I walked along the sidewalk, parallel to them. Still feigned ignorance while witnessing it all from the storefront window reflection. A massive brother who seemed impossible to have fit inside hustled toward the Benz. Was too warm for the jacket he was wearing, which could be used to hide something.

As he came around the front of Mrs. Roy's ride, I darted into the street behind him. Mindful that a hail of gunfire from within the Suburban could erupt at me at any time, I was sure to move in as non-threatening a manner as possible.

"Say, bruh! Y'all need a jump?" I asked, smiling widely as I caught up before he'd made it to her driver's door. The fuckin' bear looked to weigh at least twice as much as me. Why was I always running up against monsters like this?

"Nah. Nah. We good," he said, frowning as he tried to make out my face from beneath my pulled-down cap. I kept tilting and angling my head away from him and any of his friends in the Suburban that might be watching.

"Okay, cause I got some cables in my bag right here," I uttered, still smiling as I slipped my backpack around from off my shoulder then stuck my right hand inside. I got closer to him. Too close for sanity. Then standing on my tiptoes to get in his face, grunted in not as friendly a manner as before, "Because if nothing's wrong with your ride, then you and your boys need to move on. Now."

Without removing my hand, I pushed my backpack against his profound gut. Let him feel the protruding electronics inside, his mind painting a picture of what it might be my hand rested on inside.

"Is something wrong?" Mrs. Roy asked, getting out of her car at the wrong fucking time. I kept my eyes on my new friend.

"No, ma'am. He's just about to move out your way," I replied, pushing my backpack against him a little more firmly now.

"You don't know who you fuckin' with, li'l nigga," he said low enough for only me to hear.

"Just leave. Before this gets real messy real quick. Starting with your big ass. And don't think I'm alone," I stressed. Took great joy in watching his squinty eyes jet from side to side, suddenly wary of all the cars parked along the sidewalk. Wondering what kind of threat they posed.

I backed off, positioning myself between him and a still complaining Mrs. Roy. His move now.

An equally false smile broke on his face as he made the prudent choice and began heading back to the Suburban. But not without a parting shot of his own.

"Mrs. Roy, tell your husband we said, 'Hi,'" he mouthed before somehow fitting himself back inside the SUV.

I was right. This was to have been a message for her husband. Had Mr. Smith hired somebody else, hoping the best one succeeded? Or was this a wild card?

I didn't move until the SUV drove off. Felt a hand come to rest on my shoulder, but still didn't turn around.

"Thank you, sir," she said.

"You're welcome, ma'am. What was that about?" I asked, playing the naïve Good Samaritan who happened along.

"Just some thugs. Trying to intimidate my husband through me. But I won't let them win. He's got more important things to worry about," she replied. Tough one. Voice was sexy, too.

"I'm Taralynn. Pleased to meet you," she said. Just waiting for me to turn and face her. Shit. More of a big deal if I didn't.

I turned around, quickly responding with, “Hi. I’m—”

“Truth?” she called out before I could make up a name, leaving me speechless.

I’d dared to turn around.

And I knew her.

I knew the DA’s wife.

But, worse yet, she knew me.

This fuckin’ town.

18

Days Gone By
New Orleans

"What do you think, Truth?" she asked after she pushed pause on the CD player.

"It's good," I simply said, focused more on the apple I was slicing. At least I wanted her to think that.

"Good? Nigga, you ain't 'bout shit," she scoffed as she pranced around the picnic table. Her voice had magical powers. Made most people do things. Like throw money at her, promise her the moon . . . and do anything to possess her.

And I hadn't even gotten to how pretty she was. One of them high yella girls who came from an established New Orleans family, but bucked their carefully laid plans for her. Spent more time instead in the clubs and bars trying to be discovered, which isn't hard when you're a five-foot-ten black girl with blue-gray eyes in Tipitina's or the tourist traps on Bourbon Street.

In short, she was a good look for the face of any record label.

Women wanted to be her and the fellas wanted to be with her. A winning formula for record sales. Something Jason had discussed as desperately needed for On-Phire.

She went by the name of Still Summer, influenced by her poetry 'cause she had that fire and her sound was hot year round. I just called her Summer. Jason said she was imitating the two-name thing like that singer Truth Hurts, but that he was going to work on changing hers once we had her locked down with a long-term deal.

"If I ain't 'bout shit, then why is my opinion so valuable?" I teased as I held up an apple slice on the end of my blade and pointed it at her.

"'Cause you're the only one that never says anything about my songs. About my music. Not even a smile from you when I'm in the booth," she said as she snatched the slice away and plopped it in her mouth. "Is that too much to ask?"

"It's not my job to critique the talent. North is the talent evaluator."

"What is your job? What do you do . . . besides stand around?"

"Security," I answered, lying. Just like the man I called my uncle was teaching me. "I'm there to make sure everybody's safe."

"I don't feel safe, Truth," she said as she stared out onto Lake Pontchartrain. Vulnerability wasn't something she normally showed. "You're doing a shitty job."

I smiled finally. "Then why you here with me?" I asked. Here was Lake Terrace Park after a power outage led to cutting her studio session short. So no one would suspect, I'd met up with her down the street then we drove here together.

"I like you. You're not like the rest of them. Especially Melvin," she said, referring to the real money and the power behind On-Phire Records. "I ain't no scaredy bitch, but he scares me with those eyes. Wish Jason would tell him to stay away."

"He can't. Melvin's a business partner, so you might as well get used to him being around," I offered. "He's On-Phire as much as North is." And besides, Melvin could have Jason North killed if ever pissed off. Wouldn't be the first notch on his kill-a-nigga-dead belt. But I wasn't going to share that with her. My job was to see where her head was. Jason, always the schemer, had noticed her curiosity in me. Didn't discourage it.

"You think Melvin had something to do with AK . . ."

"No," I said, swiftly cutting her off. She's lucky she said it to me and not in front of anyone else. AK, our biggest rap act, had just been killed. Gunned down on the West Bank by a crazy-ass NOPD officer last week. Jason and Melvin had a contract dispute with AK, so it would be logical to assume they had something to do with it. But they were innocent just this once. Even paid for a nice wreath at the funeral.

Summer walked around to my side of the picnic table. Long legs fit into a pair of tight shorts found a spot next to me and slid right in. Nothing said as she rested her head on my shoulder.

I checked my watch as I felt my heart racing, an annoying feeling. Would've loved staying out here on the lake with her all day. All night too. But being a horny kid had no place in this. Never had time to be a kid anyway, so why start now.

"Power's probably on now at the studio. I should be getting you back," I said.

"Why? Because they told you?"

"No. Because you have a job to do. And so do I," I replied as I forced myself to stand. Hoped I sounded convincing.

"What is your job, Truth? To watch me for your bosses? To keep me happy?"

"Whatchu think?" I shot back as I stowed my knife. Began walking back toward the car. But she grabbed my wrist.

"So . . . keep me happy," she said, eyes afire.

Like it was still summer.

In the back seat of my old Impala off Lakeshore Drive, I did my best to make Summer happy. My pants dropped to my ankles. Her shorts and panties cast away in the front seat. Wasn't my first time, but damn sure felt like it in terms of the excitement that gripped me. Probably just the fear of being caught out here in broad daylight like this.

But I liked it.

Would never say I loved her. Love was something foreign. Just a word that usually set you up for great hurt. But intense "like" was enough to fill me from head to toe with little electric tingles 'n' shit. As I went about fucking that good pussy, wanted to fill her with that same feeling. Needed her to really like me for the moment. With one of those long legs of hers resting against the headrest and the other one stuck in the air, her foot pressed into the ceiling, she met my unyielding lust with a fervor of her own.

I stroked her deep, stroked her good. Made her cum repeatedly, sweet passion sweeping her face as she held on to my hips. Guided and tugged me into her, assisting my thrusts as she led me to my finish.

"Oooh, oooh, mmmm," she moaned. "C'mon. That's it. Love me."

I pressed against her, lowering myself from the potential view of onlookers as I fucked her more vigorously. Kissed her firmly as Summer began kicking her legs, floodgates wide open as she convulsed on the car seat beneath me.

"I . . . I," I grunted, sweat forming on my face as I struggled to breathe.

"Uh huh," was all she said, flashing those eyes as she nodded for me join her in her ecstasy.

And I did.

An uncontrollable eruption of my essence, the electric tingles overwhelming me into uselessness. We lay there across my back seat with our fingers intertwined, our breathing engaged in a slowly fading race. And foolishly looking into one another's eyes.

"What are we doing?" I asked, once I had sufficient strength to voice it. Spontaneity was something I was unaccustomed to.

"Uh . . . having fun, silly," she answered for me.

"True," I responded, kissing her again. "But we really need to go now."

"I know, I know," she agreed this time.

"Go on in. I'll be there in a second," I said as I came to a stop outside the Gentilly Boulevard recording studio we were using. Had stopped at my place and quickly cleaned up. If pressed, I was going to blame our delay on a traffic accident.

"Wanna get rid of that smile from this lovin', huh? Ain't mad atcha," Summer joked before she gave me a kiss on the cheek. "Go 'head and get your hard face back on. I won't tell."

I knew she wouldn't. We'd agreed on the way here that it was just a one-time thing. Any regret that I felt over the agreement, I kept to myself.

When I saw she was safely inside, I took a deep breath. Nervous about the act to which I'd committed. An act of which Summer was unaware. And of which Jason was totally unaware.

I called someone.

"Is you daughter Summer? Still Summer?" I asked when someone answered. Was steady watching my mirrors in case someone was walking up.

"Yes. That's what she calls herself. Who is this?" the obviously irritated man asked.

"Just listen. Your daughter is associating with the wrong crowd. Signed a recording contract. Do whatever's necessary to break it."

"Young man, my daughter is not one to listen. So just how am I supposed to do that?"

"She has a contract with On-Phire Records. If you push hard enough, they won't push back. Too much trouble and you have the money to put up a fight. Do what everyone else does. Hire a good lawyer. Maybe your daughter was seventeen when she signed her first contract and maybe someone changed a date or something. Look there. But don't let her stay with them. They're dangerous. If you love her," I said, wielding that foreign word love, before continuing, "you'll do whatever it takes."

I hung up after that. Now it was on him. Closed my flip phone and went back inside the studio. An intimate crowd of label mates and some local media had gathered to hear On-Phire's latest artist. An attempt to move the news cycle on from the rapper AK's death.

"All good, Truth?" Jason asked, wearing a charcoal sport coat and fresh from his law practice on Elysian Fields Avenue. As I took my place in the back of the room, he grinned inside the confines of his goatee. He knew I'd been out with Summer.

"Yeah," I said as he patted me on the back. From inside the booth, Summer winked at me as she donned her headphones. "It's all good."

Jason wanted me to get a read on her.

Well, I did.

Had a read on him too.

This was my first time going against his plans and wishes.

Didn't know at that time, but it wouldn't be my last.

19

"Truth," she uttered again as if she had trouble believing it and had to convince herself.

Wanted to grant her wish and deny my very existence right to her lying eyes.

But I couldn't.

Not standing here, facing her on Magazine Street.

"Summer?" I asked of the face I remembered so well, but assumed I'd never see again. Someone had taken the wild young thang I knew, painting it with the brush of experience that only time can give. Those bluish gray eyes still were dazzling, but they were tamed. Tempered. Cultured.

With hair that was pinned up, her costume to the world consisted of a white blouse with pearls around her neck and a gray skirt with black belt. Legs were still on display, honed from time in the gym no doubt.

"Is it really you?" she asked, my less-than-ideal appearance giving her pause.

"Uh . . . yeah," I responded as the wide smile of hers surfaced. Not the conditions under which I'd want a reunion.

"What . . . what are you doing here? How long have you been back?" Summer peppered at me. Then she extended her hands, wanting to embrace, but awkwardly choosing not to.

“Was just going for a walk,” I vaguely answered. “Haven’t been back too long. Small world, huh? You . . . you look good.” I said, choosing to end on an honest note.

“Thanks,” she said, blushing. But still blocking traffic. “I . . . I need to move. Let me give you a ride. It’s the least I could do.”

Curiosity and courtesy dictated that I accept. No way that she could’ve known I’d been following her from English Turn. Hell, I didn’t know I was following her either.

We sat inside the little corner turquoise building, half a mile down Magazine from where we started. We were seated in the window of Guy’s Po-Boys, a clear view of her Mercedes parked curbside in case her number-one fans returned. A bite to eat while her daughter was at ballet practice was my suggestion. Easier to distract her with my genuine hunger rather than trying to cook up a destination for my alleged walk.

“Married?” she asked. Still was blunt.

“No. Not as lucky as you,” I replied as our hot sandwiches—a hot sausage for me and a grilled chicken for her—were brought to our table by the waiter. Summer insisted on paying for it and I knew better than to let my pride show.

She splashed a dash of hot sauce on her sandwich and her side of potato salad, methodical in her approach. Could tell life was now an ordered affair for her. “I heard about Jason dying in Monaco. Thought about you. And my wild days,” she said, a nervous chuckle as she poured a few packets of Splenda in her tea and stirred. “You’re not still tied up with the label are you?”

“Nooo. Left that long ago,” I said, savoring the good eats.

"So what do you do?" Summer asked as she glanced up.

"Odd jobs," I replied as a bunch of variables were firing off in my head. Her seeing me like this, had to figure I was down on my luck. Had seen better days. Although she was too nice to admit it, a figure that she once desired was now only worthy of her pity.

If she only knew.

She chuckled. "Same old Truth. Not one for more than a syllable or two."

"What do you do?" I asked, playing my part. "I mean . . . besides pushing a Mercedes, which you do so well."

"I'm a mother, housewife . . . busy with the links and community projects too."

"Wow," I responded, wiping my mouth. "Just like your parents wanted for you, right?"

"Fuck you, Truth," she shot back, giving me the side eye, but with a disarming smile.

I wagged my finger. Started to bring up that fleeting moment on Lake Pontchartrain all those years gone by. But didn't. "You still sing some?" I queried instead, for various reasons.

"No. That was then. My father got me away from On-Phire. Then things happened after that . . . Life 'n' stuff," she said, looking out the window, seeing something that wasn't really there. "Made it through college though. Loyola. Then marriage. So . . . what brings you back to town?"

I'm here to kill your husband. "A friend needed me, so I came back," I answered.

"Uh huh. Is this friend male or female?"

"Cute. One of my boys is doing renovations. Helping him paint 'n' stuff."

"That's what's in your bag?" she asked about the backpack I kept near me. "Your tools?"

"Yep," I said about the electronic surveillance equipment. "That and clothes."

Torn between wanting to know all about her new life and mining for intel to rip her staid life apart, I went with the job.

"What was that about back there with the fat man? What did he want with your husband?"

"Boy, you really haven't been around. My husband's the DA. Youngest one in New Orleans ever," she said, genuinely proud of his accomplishments.

I mock applauded. "Look at you, Still Summer," I teased. I'd put her on this path long ago. Saving her from certain exploitation at the hands of Jason North and Melvin. Not knowing that I'd come back into her idyllic life one day . . . to destroy it.

"Ugh. Please don't call me that. Haven't used that name in forever."

"What should I call you then?" I asked, already knowing the answer.

"Taralynn," she answered.

"Beautiful name."

"And what's your real name?"

"Truth. That's my real name."

"Get the fuck outta here," she remarked. Reminded me more of Still Summer than Taralynn. "I always thought that was made up."

"Nope. My momma had a wicked sense of humor. What's your daughter's name? And any photos?"

"Sasha," Summer . . . I mean Taralynn said. "And of course I have photos."

She reached in her Coach purse, retrieving a matching wallet. Produced a photo of her little ballerina, which she handed across the table to me.

"Wow. Such a cutie. Tall. But she gets all that from her momma," I said as I handed back the photo of the little ballerina who was an innocent in the games of a man I knew only as Mr. Smith.

"Thank you. Sasha has exceptional talent. Just have to keep nurturing that talent."

"How old is she?"

Taralynn paused as she placed the photo back in the wallet then returned the wallet to her purse. "Nine," she replied as she lowered the Coach to the floor once again.

"Wow. She is tall," I said with a smile. "But moving on to her daddy the DA, do people try to leave *messages* for him through you on the regular? I mean . . . you're lucky I happened to be around."

"Yeah. I guess I was lucky," she said, eyeing me suspiciously. Wondered if I'd tipped my hand by being too pushy with the narrative. "Kinda like when somebody called my dad back in my Still Summer days. Told him all about On-Phire. And that he needed to get me outta that sitch. Know anything about that, Truth?"

"Nah," I said, taking a sip of my Coke. "On-Phire had a bunch of enemies and unhappy folk within the camp back then. Coulda been anyone."

"Uh huh," she uttered, fire flaring into those eyes. Then she looked at her watch, moving her along from whatever she was going to say. "I have to get back to the dance studio. If you'd like, I can give you that ride after I pick up Sasha."

"Nah. I'm good. Need to stretch my legs after all this food. Besides the job I'm working on is in the area."

"Y'know," she said as she grabbed her purse and prepared to leave. "I believe in paying things forward. My husband and I have been blessed and have a ton of connections, Truth. Could hook you up with a nice job. Good pay. *Benefits*. What do you say, old friend?"

"I appreciate it, but I'm good. Really," I replied. She honestly thought me at the mercy of the world.

"Well, we're going to have to continue catching up later. Okay?"

"Bet," I said.

We exchanged numbers, Taralynn giving me a kiss on the cheek then zipping out the door to pick up her daughter as I ordered another Coke.

We'd be talking again.

Soon.

For I needed any inside info on Rodney Roy to get this job over with.

One thing I realized though.

I couldn't kill him.

20

"How are things progressing?" Mr. Smith asked.

"On the ground. Getting a lay of the land. Place is . . . *complicated* to say the least. Still trying to figure out why the area they call the West Bank is south of the city," I replied, almost certain he was unaware of my connection to the N.O.

"No time for that. Finish the job. Or I finish you."

"Can you at least tell me why?" I asked as I looked up at the cloudy sky and the large object passing overhead that held my attention.

"I'm about to hang up."

"You know he has a family, right?"

". . . Do it. This week. I'll know if you don't," Mr. Smith said in conclusion. From his hesitation, I knew he had a family himself. Was constructing a nice profile of the motherfucker.

I checked my phone app for incoming flight schedules seeing that the one I was expecting had arrived on time. I was waiting in the Hilton parking lot across Airline Drive from the airport while entertaining Mr. Smith, but now it was time to move. I put the rented Mazda in gear and headed out.

As I rolled through the passenger pickup/baggage lane, I saw the person for whom I was there. Standing around in one of those busy, fitted T-shirts and jeans while conversing with another traveler. A quick call and they answered.

"Yo," they said.

"Little black Mazda," I calmly recited from behind my black sunglasses.

"Oh. I see you."

"One other thing."

"What?"

"Lose the bird that's trying to give you the digits. Not that kind of trip," I tersely instructed as I inched up with the stop-and-go flow of traffic. When I got close enough, I popped the trunk, allowing them to deposit their luggage. Then they joined me.

"Can't believe you're doing this for me. But I appreciate it," Ivan Dempsey said, plopping into the passenger seat and flashing his practiced, perfect smile. "Damn. You didn't prepare me for the humidity down here. Nuts stickin' to my jeans 'n' shit. Would've worn some shorts."

"You didn't tell Sophia, right?" was my response to his pleasantries as I sped away from the airport.

"No. But she's gonna worry when I don't come home. My P.O. might trip too."

"Don't worry about Sophia. She's a big girl. And your parole officer will continue to file his regular reports on you."

"Damn. Got it like that, huh? Sophia said you're the shit. How much does this pay?"

"Your share?"

"Yeah. Whatever," he corrected with a sneer.

"Enough for you to leave Sophia alone and never look back."

"You'd like that."

"Doesn't matter what I like. It's how it's gonna be if you want the money."

"Fuck the cloak and dagger, black man. What am I supposed to be doing for this money?"

"Murder," I calmly mouthed as I got on I-10 to head toward downtown.

"Nah. Hell nah. I just got out. You can pull over now and I'll find my own way back to Cali."

"C'mon, Ivan," I said with a dismissive chuckle. "Don't act like you haven't killed before. What was it? Your sixth month in there? That guy you shanked in the shower for the Russians in order to get their protection. I know Sophia doesn't know about that. Or about why you needed their protection. How bad did they stretch that asshole, pretty boy?"

Ivan clenched his jaw. Some of what I said was speculation, but he didn't deny it. "I should kill you," he said.

"You could try. I might like that, but I gotta keep my mind on business."

"Why me?" he asked, most resistance having already faded from his words.

"When I said models follow instruction well, I meant it," I said, reaching under my seat without taking my eyes off the road. We were going through Metairie, neighborhood sound barrier walls on display on both sides of I-10, and heading toward the infamous Seventeenth Street canal whose levee burst after Katrina. Of course, it ruptured on the Orleans Parish side. At the I-10/I-610 split, I fetched $20,000 of fresh bills and tossed the bound currency into Ivan's lap. "And because I know this is just a little taste of what awaits you when this job is over."

Sun Tzu said, "If they are greedy, lure them with goods. Show them a little prospect of gain to lure them, then attack and overcome them."

"I see," he muttered. Could tell he regretted even entertaining my proposal. But he was hungry. Mind probably fantasizing about what illicit substances he could snort, shoot, and smoke with what rested in his lap. Would have to keep an eye on him.

"I'm bringing you to the W. Already have a room there. Just need you to hang out for now. Enjoy the food. Do some gambling at Harrah's with what I just gave you. Maybe you'll get lucky. Just don't be calling Sophia."

"Who am I supposed to be killing?" he asked as his thumb continued to graze the edges of the stacks.

"A lawyer. That's all," I said half truthfully with a smile meant to put him at ease. "Everybody hates lawyers."

Using one problem to solve another, I thought smugly.

21

Could've just sicced Ivan on Rodney already. Aimed him like a mindless missile at the DA. Boom. Mission accomplished. I had the *how,* but I still wanted to know the *why*.

Didn't have time to stage a place, so I found one on Delachaise Street suitable for my needs. Once picked, I had a go-between pose as a film company rep, paying the occupants for their inconvenience and sending them on an all-expense-paid trip to Walt Disney World while their home was used for the shoot. Funny that the Williams family would spend the next year bragging about their house being featured in a movie that never was.

Took half a day to rearrange and personalize, but I was just in time. There came a knock at the door, but I waited until the second one to respond.

"Hello," I said, smiling widely as I opened the door wearing a white T-shirt, Nike shorts, and socks.

"Hey," Taralynn said as she stood on the porch of the shotgun house. "Well, I'm here," she added, waiting for her invite. The neighbor across the street, an elderly lady in a housecoat with a wig and sunglasses for no fucking reason, was looking suspiciously at the two strangers she'd never seen until today.

"Come on in," I said as I waved at the neighbor, pretending it was all good for Taralynn's benefit. My new neighbor was still frowning as I closed the door.

Based on our first encounter, I had arranged the interior a step above her notions and a step below what I considered my worst. I offered her a seat, seeing that as she lowered herself into the skinny sofa, she was dressed a lot less formal than last time. The purple hoodie and black yoga pants she wore were as if she didn't want anybody to recognize her as the "DA's wife." But I didn't know her like that these days and it was a woman's prerogative to switch up her look. No matter. Dressed up or dressed down, she was still smokin'.

"So this is where you live, huh?" she asked as she looked around, keeping her face neutral.

"Yeah. A roof over my head. And the air works. But once I save up enough money, I'll probably move," I said, feigning embarrassment over my less-than-stellar accommodations. If I'd invited her to my room at the Holiday Inn, she probably would've thought I was trying to fuck her. Not that it couldn't happen here, if that were my intention. "Want anything to drink? I have water, Barq's, beer, wine," I offered.

"No thanks. I'm good."

"Well . . . glad you could make it," I said as I sat across from her in a chair I tried pretending great comfort with.

"Rodney's at the office again preparing for his case. And Sasha's at the Audubon Zoo with her friends, so I had a little bit of free time. You're lucky you caught me. Now . . . what was so urgent?" she asked.

"I . . . I just . . . It was so strange running into you the other day and honestly . . . well. It was rushed and awkward, so I just wanted to see you again," I said as I scooted to the edge of my seat.

"Awww," she responded, taken aback. "That's very sweet of you, Truth. You've certainly mellowed."

"Maybe a little. But still protective of you."

"Oh, that," Taralynn muttered, rolling her eyes. "Still worried about that guy you ran off?"

"I won't even pretend to know about your husband and what he does," I started, "but if somebody's threatening you on the street, I'd take that seriously. I used to run with cats like that, remember? I have no right, but . . ."

"Yeah. You don't," she said, repositioning herself on the uncomfortable sofa with an uneven leg. "Believe it or not, you sound a lot like my husband. If he had his way, police would be with me twenty-four-seven, but you know the old me ain't havin' that. Fear is not an option."

"Not for Still Summer, but Taralynn has more than herself to be concerned about. How about for your daughter? I'm sure she wants her mother *and* her father to be around for a long time."

She stood up. Straight popped out her seat like a spring was under her ass. "Don't bring Sasha into this! That's some dirty shit you're pulling and you have no right, Truth!" she raged as she towered over me, the protective mother borrowing the *fire* of Summer's past. Sometimes pushing buttons can blow up in your face. And I had a serious case of emotional dynamite on my hands.

"Whoa. Easy," I said, shielding myself half seriously. "I was just trying to point out another way of looking at things. Didn't call you here to upset you. I'm sorry."

"All right then," she said, apparently satisfied. "And I apologize for snapping on you like that. I try not to think negatively because I'd lose my mind, but this upcoming trial of Rodney's does have me stressing. I . . . I'm not sleeping like I should. I'm cranky."

"Well, sit back down and let me get you a glass of wine."

Had a cheap brand chilling in the fridge. Smooth tasting, but with enough alcohol to get her pliable. Poured us both a glass then sat next to her. Just a shoulder to lean on; a sounding board if she wanted to get something off her chest. Didn't expect her to down the first glass so fast, but maybe being in my presence made her more nervous than I thought. Was over a decade since we were intimate, but those connections don't just disappear. As I began massaging her neck, I pressed on.

"What kind of trial does your husband have coming up? Murder?" I asked.

"Yeah. That and criminal conspiracy," she said as she closed her eyes and moaned in agreement with what I was doing with my fingers. "Some big-time drug dealer from off Earhart . . . Braxton Lewis. Will be glad when it's over."

"And you think that's what fat man was about on Magazine?"

"Yep," she said with a sigh. "Rodney's busting his ass to clean things up around here. Makes for a shitload of enemies. Y'know . . . this Braxton Lewis reminds me a lot of Melvin from our old On-Phire days. God, I used to be so scared of that man. I'm glad both of us were able to escape that camp," Taralynn said as she lazily dropped her hand on my knee.

"Yeah . . . me too," I said as I stopped massaging her neck and looked into her eyes. Our foreheads touched and remained there. Got so dialed into extracting info that I'd gotten too comfortable with her for my own good. Killing her husband would be fucking her enough.

"Um . . . I think I need to be going. Because this is probably not the best look for me being here," she said ever so softly as she smartly retreated. "And me and you got . . ."

"Yeah. I know," I commented with a polite smile. "History."

After making sure Taralynn was sober enough to drive and giving her some water to take with her, I walked her outside to her SUV.

"It was good seeing you, Summer," I voiced, knowing I was exposing myself to a punch or an elbow. But she refrained. Stayed ladylike. She would need that resolve in the coming days.

"Likewise, Truth," she said as she started the SUV. Jennifer Hudson was playing on her stereo. "Don't be a stranger."

"I won't," I replied.

As the GLK drove off, I was already on my phone, establishing a secure link.

Hey. Need a favor, I texted.

Yeah. Yeah. No speak 4 like a year then . . .

Frustrated, I ended the conversation and simply called, violating protocol.

"You're actually calling?" Lorelei Smart, the owner of the Web site 4Shizzle answered, knowing the blocked call had to be me.

"I'm desperate," I said, knowing our last communication had been when I was in South Beach. The night I was shot.

"Go on," she said.

"I need whatever you can pull up on a New Orleans drug dealer by the name of Braxton Lewis. Family members, et cetera."

"Braxton Lewis. Ain't he on trial?"

"Wow," I responded, impressed. "You know about that?"

"Hey. I peddle in more than just gossip. Be impressed," she crowed. "You can't do this yourself? I normally get my intel and scoop from you, not the other way around."

"I would, but I don't have time. Kinda pushed into something last minute."

"And what do I get?" Lorelei cooed.

"A story. Like the old days. If I live."

"Cryptic. I want a fuckin' story even if you die," she joked.

"Deal."

"How soon?"

"Tonight," I said, hearing the clock ticking in my head courtesy of Mr. Smith.

Very soon, I was going to have to turn Ivan loose.

If a new wing was opening for me in hell, I at least wanted to know the layout.

22

"Uh . . . think you can spot me some more? Kinda need it for this place, bro," he said as we sat in the parking lot, neon lights flashing through the windshield.

I handed Ivan another ten Gs. Asked, "What happened to what I gave you?"

"Gone at Harrah's. Easy come, easy go, bro," he said cavalierly. "Besides, it's the tip of the iceberg anyway, right?" The tip I was worried about was the tip of his nose diving into that white girl. I wasn't stupid. Harrah's only accounted for some of the money he'd blown through.

And I cringed every time he called me "bro." Other than Sophia's pussy, I shared nothing in common with him. Where I was chess, he was hopscotch. A basic conman who relied on his looks and smooth tongue, but not a lot between his ears. Maybe I envied him for not having the burden of thought.

"Yeah. You're right," I responded, false smile evident. "And there might be more jobs after this." Decided to curb my obvious dislike for the man. Play nice for my purposes. Make him think opportunities abounded.

"Word?" he greedily uttered. "My man! Uh . . . I still gotta stay away from Sophia?"

"Yeah. But I think what's inside will make you forget," I said as I motioned toward the front of Fancy's Gentlemen's Club on Chef Menteur Highway. A steady line of customers was already formed at the iron-barred security door.

"Ain't no forgettin' Sophia. But I appreciate it," he said, hopping out the car like a jackrabbit.

Despite the promise of money, knew he had no intention of staying away from Sophia. But as long as he believed that I believed him, he'd do what I said.

As I exited to catch up with an overeager and probably coked-up Ivan, I was still digesting what had me out here.

With 4Shizzle's help, I'd learned many rap stars with New Orleans roots held reverence or at least begrudging respect for Braxton Lewis or "Bricks" as he was known in the dope game. A lifelong resident of New Orleans, originally from the Earhart area, but now living in New Orleans East, Bricks was rumored to be in bed with the Mexican cartels, supplying New Orleans and the rest of the Gulf Coast with the finest grade of Colombian white. Ivan would be a true fan of him if he knew.

Where Bricks messed up was when he let his temper get the best of him. After losing a game of pool at a sports bar, Bricks and his boys followed the unfortunate victim to a New Orleans Original Daiquiris and Bricks personally worked him over on the parking lot, putting two to the head for good measure in front of several witnesses. Of course, most developed sudden amnesia and refused to testify when they realized who it was, but there were still too many to intimidate or coerce.

Now it looked like Mr. Rodney Roy was one DA who couldn't be intimidated or coerced either, putting together a serious case for Bricks where life in prison loomed. And with the trial scheduled to begin next week, this Braxton Lewis was the reason Mr. Smith needed the DA dead. Had to be.

But how was it personal for Mr. Smith, a guy who did clandestine things on behalf of the good ol' U.S. of A. and who probably didn't live in Louisiana?

His relationship to Bricks was a lingering puzzle piece that I couldn't make fit.

But I would.

Avoiding the surveillance cameras on the outside getting a clear shot of my face, both Ivan and I rolled up in the joint sporting tailored suits, designer watches, and Italian shoes. *All black everything* as Jay-Z would say, dressed on another level compared to the other clientele and wanting to smell of not just money, but power. Before I picked up Ivan and dragged him here under the pretense of just showing him a good time, I had one of my stripper contacts in Vegas put me in touch with one of her girls here at Fancy's. Had her get all the girls hyped over a big spender she knew was coming to town.

Although the shadows were my thing, sometimes it paid to be the firecracker in the library. A bright light drawing all the moths in, so I could find the right one and pick it off.

Center stage of the club was arranged as a cross in the middle of the floor. Ironically appropriate in heavily Catholic New Orleans. But for all the sinning taking place here tonight, it would take more than a few Hail Marys for absolution. Two strippers took the stage as we sat, regulars applauding as Mizz New Orleanz and DarkNLovely gyrated to Lil Wayne and later dropping and shaking to Waka Flocka Flame.

Rather than joining Ivan and the rest of them at the stage's end, where money was flying freely, I stayed seated. Waited for the moths.

"Hope you're waiting for me to take the stage," a woman in black leather boots and matching bikini uttered as she seductively sat in my lap and put her arm around me. Sister had a beauty mark on her left cheek, the left ass cheek.

"How'd you guess?" I asked, admiring her body. For real. She was a walking felony.

"Because you look like the type that knows what he wants . . . and they ain't it," she said with a wink and nod toward her two coworkers on stage. I watched the other men watch her as she whipped her hair, two different shades of brown, around.

"Ralph," I said as I took her hand and kissed it.

"You always a gentleman, Ralph?"

"If it helps me get what I want," I flirted as I placed a hundred dollar bill in her bra. "Maybe we can see where it takes us later in the VIP."

"All right, big money," she said, removing the money as she stood up to leave. "If you're still around when I finish my set, maybe we'll see."

As my friend took the stage, the DJ announcing her as Ron DMC, her own special entrance music played. Was a fusion of bounce and horns that got the men standing and hollering. I tried to just sit there and not be impressed, but she was bad. She strutted down the center runway, setting the titties free as she snapped her leather top off and flung it. Slid across the floor, rolling onto her back which she arched as she put her legs in the air and pulled off her panties. Those, she flipped overhead into the crowd. Must have been hard for the other dancers knowing Ron DMC could have their men if she ever wanted. She took to the pole, swinging around with such force as if she'd launch through the air. But she didn't. Held it strong with a command that the other dancers would die for.

While the main show went on, Ivan was working on Mizz New Orleanz and some of her friends, drawing the easy pickings in with his advance for a job that wasn't actually paying. But he was worth the money to be rid of him. A couple of others, including DarkNLovely, stayed back, feeling some of the other customers might be equally rewarding. Watched them play the game—a smile here, a touch there, all geared toward getting those dollars out those wallets. Several walked by, but none came up to me despite the thirsty faces. Was like I'd been marked with an invisible sign.

"'Bout to hit up the VIP, bro. You good?" Ivan asked with two lovelies on his arms. Probably wondering why I wasn't copping a handful of ass or squeezing a breast or two.

"Yeah. I'm more than good. Talk to you later."

Ivan left for his private session, casually flipping some of his bills behind him like a fuckin' yellow brick road for the vultures to swoop up. As he got out my hair, I smiled at the woman on stage. With DJ Drama's "Oh My" playing, she touched her toes while her ass quaked. Looking at me upside down and with money raining onto the stage, she smiled back.

I was back on why I was here when Ron DMC finished her set and came to see me, wearing nothing but a silk robe and her leather boots.

"Ready for that VIP?" she asked as she held out her hand, a fresh bottle of champagne in the other one.

"Sandy said she heard about you from her friends in Vegas," Ron DMC commented while she worked her ass round and round in my lap. She had ditched her leather boots and fierce demeanor. Was all soft and sensual now for my entertainment.

"Yeah. So?" I mumbled, shirt unbuttoned and pulled from out my pants. Was ready to pull something else out.

"Nothin'," she replied as she slowly stroked my dick through my pants with those incredible cheeks of hers. Up and down against a pole of a different sort as she bent over. Pants were damp, but couldn't tell if it was more from me or more from her. She suddenly fell back, flipping her hair across my face to Kelly Rowland's "Motivation." Letting me hold her by the waist as she wound her body like a snake across the landscape that was me. "I like men of means. Motherfuckers with that swag. They make me cum. You wanna make me cum, Ralph?" she asked, panting in my ear.

"Yeah, yeah. I do," I answered as I caressed her taut stomach, moving my hands downward across her thighs while trying to think. That's it. Think. And not about my hard-on.

The puzzle.

Braxton Lewis had two siblings, a brother and a sister. The brother, Rontrell, was gunned down three years ago on A.P. Tureaud Avenue. Some people say the man Bricks killed at the daiquiri place was the trigger man in his brother's unsolved murder. Guess nobody will ever know unless Bricks talked.

But Bricks also had a sister who was alive and healthy.

And possessing a healthy ass that could do all sorts of thangs.

Of course, she went by Ron DMC or Ron Da Mighty Coochie while working; Ron being short for Veronica.

Veronica Lewis.

If you weren't from around here or knee-deep in the case, you wouldn't know Veronica was Brick's sister. Or that she ran this business enterprise while her brother was indisposed. It was none of your business. To most customers, she was just the featured attraction.

But the fat fucker who guarded the entrance to the VIP area knew better.

He was the same one who tried to deliver the message to Taralynn.

23

I had to call Mr. Smith tonight when I left here. And with the result not yet achieved, he wouldn't like my report.

Led me to do something rash.

Had to complete the puzzle.

"Any family?" I asked, opening my eyes to look down at her.

"You really trying to kill the mood, ain'tcha?" Veronica Lewis said, down on her knees and about to unbuckle my pants with her teeth.

"Just a little conversation. That's all. You intrigue me," I said as I ran my fingers through her hair, staring at her as if she were the most beautiful woman in the world. Was easy. I could play roles too. Just imagined her to be . . . someone else. "Indulge your customer," I prodded.

Her mouth curled up. Looked like she was about to curse me out. Then she softened. "Two kids," she said as she decided to undo my belt with her hands.

"Hmm," I said, a bit of whimsy seeping across my face. "I'd like kids one day."

"Well, why don't we work on that now, baby," she said as she unzipped me, taking my dick in her hand. She went to work, lapping up the pre-cum off its head with tiny circles of her tongue.

"Mmm. Damn, girl. Would love for you to have my baby," I said, breathing heavily from her oral stimulation. "But . . . but I need to know. You got a man?"

"Huh?"

"Your two kids. I don't want to come between you and their daddy. Because I'd want that all to myself," I played.

"Don't worry. I'm very much single. My eldest's dad is dead," she said as she traveled up my shaft with that tongue. Then she paused to complete her thought. "And my youngest's dad might as well be."

"Because he has a family already," I prodded solemnly. Was going somewhere dangerous, relying on my instincts and a wild hunch.

"You know it," she said with a chuckle as she loosened her grip on my dick to reflect. "White motherfucker. But he looks out for us and keeps the checks comin'."

"How'd you meet him? Here at the club?"

"No. He was doing work . . . with . . ." she said, her face tightening. Was on to me. And that this wasn't her normal VIP session with a big spender. "Why you askin' all this?"

"He looks out for your brother too? Right?" I pushed, tensing up.

"Huh? What the fuck did you say?"

"Bricks. Does he look out for Bricks?" I said, trying to force the puzzle piece into place with a sledgehammer as my environment turned dangerous. But I had to know.

Wiping her mouth, she sprang to her feet and backed up. Had a 9 mm with laser sight hidden on the side of the couch, which she now pointed at my dick. "Party's over. Now who in the fuck are you, bitch? Furreal," she asked harshly.

"Help . . . from your baby daddy," I said, referring to Mr. Smith as I hastily zipped my pants back up. Stayed seated though as the red dot from the laser sight still hovered there. "For your brother's situation."

"Nah. This some kinda setup. I don't know you and you sure as fuck don't know me," she said as she switched her aim to the center of my chest. She held the nine steady. No way could I get to it without her getting a shot off. I was done with being shot.

"You don't believe me," I said as I stood up, my confidence flowing again despite my being a bull's-eye for one pissed off stripper. "But I can prove it."

"Well, what's his name then?"

"Good one," I said with a laugh. "You know better than that. Especially if you know what he does. He doesn't deal in names with me. At least not his real one."

Ron DMC smiled. Her tensed trigger finger easing as I'd passed that on sheer dumb luck. "True," she agreed. "But why you here?"

"The way he . . . spoke of you. I just had to see it for myself," I said, dialing up the lust in my voice as I look her over from head to toe. "Well . . . that and to tell your boy to leave the DA's family alone," I added, deciding to do some good while I was at it.

"Who?"

"Fat boy watching the hall," I said, nudging my head. "Had to stop him the other day over on Magazine. I'm supposed to be taking care of this. And don't need any of your people trying to flex."

She backed up, keeping the handgun trained on me. Opened the door to our VIP room and stuck her head in the hall. "Ezell!" she hissed.

Big ol' Ezell came running, surprised to see the scene in front of him—a naked, but gun-wielding employer . . . and me.

Who he finally recognized.

"That's him! That's the motherfucker!" Ezell shouted as he rumbled my way. Punched me dead in my gut, doubling me over. Then a right hook that felt like a boulder dropped me atop those damn leather boots of hers.

"Ezell, stop!" she shouted as his massive foot was about to come down on my head. He complied. "Now . . . talk quick before he stomps yo' ass out."

"I'm on this job," I said, still sprawled out on the floor and looking up at the both of them. "And y'all need to back the fuck off. How else would I know to be there when big boy was trying to intimidate the DA's wife? Bush league. Coulda blown everything up."

"I'll bush league yo' ass, bitch," Ezell said as he raised that damn foot of his again.

"Ezell, stop dammit!" Veronica scolded. "Now show his ass outta here."

Ezell yanked me to my feet and almost out my shoes. Veronica grabbed her robe and got in my face, but lowered the 9 mil as she did so. "Tell your boss to let me know what he's doing next time. Oh . . . and to send me double next month if he wants to see his kid or get another taste of this. That skinny wife of his is one dumb bitch," she said with disgust.

"Can I come back to see you?" I asked, still playing my role.

"If my brother goes free, you can cum back all you like, baby," she said, licking the tip of her 9 mil. "Now get outta here and go do your fuckin' job."

Fat boy escorted me from Fancy's, slapping me upside my head for good measure as I stumbled past some clientele.

"Hmph. I know what Ron said, but don't you come 'round here no mo'," he chided not so subtly. Then he threw my suit jacket at me for good measure.

I left Ivan inside. He could party a little while longer.

I had a call to make.

The puzzle now solved in my mind.

Bricks was an *asset* of Mr. Smith's I guessed. Probably for intel he provided on the Mexican cartels to the CIA or whoever in exchange for certain elements in the government looking the other way with his dope biz. But Mr. Smith got too close to Bricks and his family. Way too close with Bricks's sister. And I could see why. Now he had a little biracial bundle of joy bouncing around New Orleans. A bundle whose origins might see the light of day and cost Mr. Smith his job, and the U.S. government a heap of embarrassment, should Bricks find his way inside the walls of Angola prison and start blabbing. Or if Veronica simply got pissed off enough.

So Mr. Smith was caught by the nuts, having to help Bricks, but not wanting to be implicated in any way. Then I came along on Mr. Smith's radar. The perfect wild card with no connection to Mr. Smith or Bricks. Perfectly disposable.

I picked up the phone, a genuine smile of my face for the first time this evening. Ready to make Mr. Smith play my game for a change.

But first, I reached into the ashtray. Snagged a remote and pushed the button. A tiny microphone was now turned on and transmitting. A microphone I'd stowed inside Ron DMC's hair as I caressed it in the VIP. Right as I looked into those eyes, pretending they were Collette's. Eventually it would fall out, get vacuumed up whenever they cleaned the place. But for now, it was recording.

Now I dialed.

"You're five minutes late," Mr. Smith said. Could imagine him somewhere in Virginia, stepping out onto the porch in the middle of a diaper change or something. "Did you do it yet?"

"No. But I have a question to ask you," I said, winding up for the big pitch.

"No. No questions. I want answers and you're not giving them to me. The DA should be *reassigned* by now. So maybe the news I have for you is coming at the right time."

"What?"

"There's been an accident. In Dallas. No . . . wait . . . Frisco," he said as he facetiously corrected himself. "Yeah. That's it. An Officer Derrick Kane was struck by a hit-and-run driver tonight while on duty. Broken leg and a concussion, but he'll live. Shame you can't protect her. Tick tock, son. Tick tock," he said just before hanging up.

Warning understood loud and clear.

I sat there, boiling over.

No way Mr. Smith was going to just let me off the hook after this. It would be either another job or the graveyard. Because he was the type of person who used people like . . .

Well . . . like me.

So it was settled.

I would kill the DA.

Then I would find Mr. Smith and kill him.

24

I tapped once on his forehead. Then again for good measure. Held a hot cup of Café du Monde's café au lait for him as his senses returned, leg still dangling off the bed. Room was a mess. But at least he made it back from Fancy's.

"How'd you get in here?" Ivan groaned from under the comforter that halfway covered him.

"It's my room," I said, flashing the extra key card to remind him.

As he sat up, he grabbed his head. Groaned as he closed his eyes. Then he slowly reopened them, probably hoping I'd disappeared.

No such luck.

"Bro, furreal? I've only had about two hours sleep."

I handed the café au lait to him. "Two hours more than me," I said.

Mizz NewOrleanz was still unconscious in the bed, size D breast implants on full display. A little white powdery residue rested on the corner of her nose as she lay there engaged in an open-mouthed snore. I shook my head at the chainsaw-like sounds she was putting out. Couldn't he put his dick in her mouth to shut her up?

"Playtime is over. Get some clothes on, get rid of your girlfriend, and meet me downstairs," I instructed.

***

I was seated in a leather chair in the Living Room of the W, reading a copy of the *Times-Picayune,* when Ivan finally made his way down. Had a view of most of the first floor including the check-in desk. Two ladies looking over a tourist map, paused to check him out as he walked by.

Models.

Wondered if they'd still ogle him if they knew all the things he'd done.

And what he was about to do.

Ivan walked up to my secluded spot, adorned in sunglasses and one of those busy shirts again, and swatted at my paper. "What the fuck, bro. Why'd you leave me last night?" he gruffly asked.

"Because something came up," I responded without looking up from my reading. "Didn't want to cock block you. Besides, you're resourceful and I knew you'd find someone to get you back here."

"Finally ready to do this? Or was it all a joke?"

"Nope, I was serious. And yep, it's time."

"Now let's get down to business," Ivan said as he took a seat to my immediate right and crouched over. "What is my cut anyway? To go away so you can have Sophia all to yourself?"

"Two hundred grand," I said, ignoring his dig about Sophia. My phone buzzed just as I lied about the money. Was a text from Sophia. Wondering if I knew of Ivan's whereabouts. I texted back that I didn't and good riddance.

"Who's gotta get got?" he asked as I deleted the message from his girlfriend.

I flipped the paper around that I'd been reading and dropped it on the table in front of him.

"You got the heart for it?" I asked as he looked at a photo of DA Rodney Roy and the accompanying article on the Braxton Lewis trial titled DA ROY PUSHES FORWARD.

"Him? The fuckin' DA?"

"Shhh. Keep your voice down," I reminded him as a child came a little too close to us.

"You said it was a lawyer," Ivan groused as he flipped the newspaper back at me.

"He *is* a lawyer, dumbass," I uttered, not bothering to hide my true feelings.

"Who wants him gone?"

"Can't say. You know better."

"Job like that, probably makes a bunch of enemies. This one has money."

"Appears so."

"And you okay with it?"

"Yup," I said, lying. "Are you?"

"Yeah . . . I guess so."

"Well let's take a walk, bro," I said as I stood up.

We rode the Algiers Ferry, having boarded at the foot of Canal Street by the Aquarium of the Americas.

"He lives on this side of the river, the West Bank. You need to learn this ferry inside and out, so you can blend in," I said to Ivan as I looked over the railing at the murky waters of the Mississippi swirling below. "Leaves from downtown at fifteen and forty-five past the hour. Leaves from Algiers on the hour and thirty past."

"The DA takes the ferry?"

"He will tomorrow," I replied, training my eyes on the Crescent City Connection casting a shadow on the water.

"But tomorrow's Sunday."

"He'll be going in," I said as I thought about the trial scheduled to begin Monday. "You just be ready. I'll call you when to expect him."

"What the fuck am I supposed to use? Knife? Gun? My looks?"

"Gun with a silencer. Head shot. There will be a distraction. Just walk up . . . pop . . . then drop it overboard," I recited, pointing at the churning wake.

"Out in the open? Damn. Why not at his crib or his office?" Ivan pleaded.

"Security details at both. Inviting trouble," I commented. "Has to be en route."

"And how am I gonna get away? Magic carpet?"

"You walk away. Two uniforms. One as a ferry worker. The other as NOPD when you leave the boat. Will have a final change waiting for you in the bathroom of the Hilton New Orleans Riverside. Then there will be a cab waiting for you on Canal Street to drive you to Baton Rouge," I said as I walked around, discretely inspecting the ferry and getting a feel what the situation might be like when everything went down. "You'll just have to change really quick. Like at a fashion show. You've done some acting too before, right?"

"Yeah. Commercials 'n' stuff . . . before I went away."

"Figured. That's good. Same thing here. Except you'll be two hundred grand richer."

"Y'know . . . I've been thinking about things, bro," he said, making me cringe. Wanted to push him over the rail and put an immediate end to his shit.

"And?" I asked, regretting my indulgence instantly.

"And I want half my money up front." Greedy bastard.

“That kind of money in this town is a bad thing,” I offered up.

“I wasn’t asking,” Ivan remarked with a smirk.

“Your coke-to-stripper ratio is already too high,” I chided dismissively.

“I got that under control,” he said, frown evident across his face.

“You mean like in Cali when you told me you were clean?”

“Look. No money, no job. I’m the one taking all the risk.”

“You’re right. Forgive me. I’m being a dick because I’m under a lot of stress,” I said, gloating inside knowing Ivan wouldn’t be walking away as cleanly as I’d conveyed. “You’ll have the half upfront by tonight.”

I patted Ivan on the shoulder for good measure, him not knowing there was another set of eyes on us.

A gentleman on the upper level who tipped his hat in response to my signal.

25

"You couldn't pick up the phone and call me, Truth?" Sophia squawked.

"I'm kinda on a job," I said as I sped down Magazine Street in my rental, Bluetooth resting in my ear.

"That government thing?" she mumbled, voice dropping an octave.

"Yeah. The one I'm stuck doing because I got caught springing you," I reminded her.

"Dang. I'm sorry."

"It's all good."

"Where are you?" she asked.

"You know better," I replied, dodging her question the same as I did a large moving truck that trying to back up just then. Bluetooth almost fell off my ear. "Just know that I'm alive. Still."

"You sure you don't know where Ivan is?" Sophia pressed.

"Didn't I text you that already? Sheesh. Count your blessings that he moved on," I said as I came to a red light at Jackson Avenue next to the Shell station. I stopped, checking my rearview mirror out of habit.

"Truth . . . you didn't kill him, did you?"

"No," I answered truthfully, having left Ivan back at the W with his firearm and more money than he deserved. "Paranoia doesn't suit you. Unless something's making you paranoid."

"What the fuck are you getting at?"

"Just what I said. Something have you a little edgier than usual?"

"Don't be riddling me, Truth. Spit it out."

"Are you high? Are you on that shit again? Clear enough for you?" I yelled, glad no one outside the car could hear me.

"Is that what this is about? You're punishing me by taking away Ivan?"

"I ain't your daddy. But I am concerned about you. And just how am I supposed to spirit someone away? You're acting like I'm all-powerful or something. If Ivan chose to flake out, that's your problem. Not mine. Maybe you should go check a crack house for him, but let me handle my motherfuckin' business."

Sophia hung up without even so much as a good-bye.

Wouldn't understand or appreciate the huge favor I was doing her anyway.

But I had an unexpected appointment to keep, so I kept it moving.

Parked around the corner from the Crescent City Dance Company and walked the rest of the way. Didn't really have time to change into what Taralynn was accustomed to seeing me wear, but left the sport coat in the Mazda. Still, was happy to let her see my *potential.*

"Sir, may I help you?" a thin, blond twenty-something asked as I entered. She was dressed in all-black dancewear and seemed startled by a brother waltzing in from off the street. Can't say I was that comfortable in this place myself, but . . .

"Uh . . . yeah. I'm here for—"

"It's okay. He's family, Samantha," Taralynn said as she walked over from the company of the other moms and grandmothers with whom she'd been conversing.

Samantha's demeanor immediately changed, going from hard and sharp to soft and mushy as she gracefully stepped aside.

"Yeah. What she said," I smugly reaffirmed to the gangly guardian as Taralynn greeted me with an embrace. Had a message that she was looking for me, telling me to stop by here if I wasn't too busy. This was going to be my last time seeing her ever so, with all arrangements set for tomorrow, I made my schedule fit.

"Well, don't you look nice," she said glowingly of my dress shirt and slacks. For a Saturday afternoon, she was still polished as ever—a draped, sleeveless black tunic and jeans with little black lace-up ankle boots.

"When I got the invite, figured I'd make myself more presentable," I offered. Better than saying I was busy planning out the murder of her husband and ran right over.

"You did that, boy. Got the other moms checking you out," she teased as her friends whispered among themselves while trying to observe their daughters through the glass viewing window. "I said you're my cousin. Want me to introduce you to them?"

"Uh . . . no. I'm good," I said with a polite smile to dull the antisocial message. "Not looking for a love connection."

"Uh huh. Knew you had someone . . . or someones," Taralynn said with an elbow to my side. "And when you clean up like this, you probably have your pick of the litter. Now see . . . when I imagined how you'd turn out, *this* is how I pictured you."

"You called me over here to try to make me blush? Damn."

"Nah. Here for final rehearsal before my baby's Boston trip. They'll be performing *Swan Lake* at the Citi

Performing Arts Center. But since you live nearby, I wanted to see you again. Share a little bit more about my life these days."

"That was nice of you," I said, torn over a dirty job now moving into the realm of sheer betrayal.

"Hey. Sharing means caring," she joked with a wink.

Taralynn led me to the viewing window where we stood on one end, watching a rainbow of young ballerinas, all with their hair in buns, going through different stages of technique, stretching, and choreography. The other ladies were still waiting for an introduction from Mrs. Rodney Roy that never came. As rude as it was, way too many people in this town had seen my true face, so no need becoming familiar with my true voice too.

"That's Sasha, there," Taralynn said softly as she tapped a manicured fingernail tip to the glass, pointing to her daughter, whom I'd already recognized from the day I was following them.

"Damn," I whispered. Still tall for her age, the nine-year-old elevated and dropped repeatedly on her tippy toes as her instructor circled. Like some hungry jungle cat mouthing something at Sasha that we couldn't hear. Shit looked painful, but she made it look easy. Effortless as she maintained her focus, face stoic and showing serious professionalism for someone of her age. Ignoring the dozen or so people watching her every move from behind the glass. The girl was clearly the star pupil of the Crescent City Dance Company. Out the corner of my eye, I saw her proud momma beaming as she should. "How long has she been doing this?" I asked Taralynn.

"Since she was three," she replied. "Don't know where all her grace came from. But she's got it. Talking about her doing a solo routine in Boston as well."

"Successful spouse. Beautiful, talented daughter. Sounds like you have the perfect family," I said, looking more at my reflection in the window than what was behind it. Wondered if I weren't damaged goods, might I have had a family like this.

"It's ain't so bad. I'll admit I've been blessed," she said, sunshine in her voice as she casually rubbed my back.

"So what's your schedule for tomorrow?" I asked as her hand still lingered. Wanted her to think it was about her when it was really about intel. Any extra bit of information that maybe I hadn't factored into my plans. Like if Taralynn and her daughter suddenly decided to accompany Daddy to work tomorrow.

Sun Tzu once said, "Only when you know every detail of the lay of the land can you maneuver and contend."

"We fly out tomorrow evening," Taralynn answered, looking away from the window to answer me eye to eye. "Staying away the whole week. For the best with Rodney's big trial taking place. It usually consumes all his time, so I like to get away with Sasha to let him focus."

"Uh huh," I said, nodding. Thinking about how it is with ambitious people who neglect their spouses. But I didn't know if this was the case with the Roys. How could I?

"You really should meet him, Truth," she said awkwardly, turning her focus back to her daughter. "Maybe we can have you over when all this dies down."

"I'd like that," I said, displaying my war mask.

26

Was back at the Holiday Inn near the Superdome, when my phone stirred me from my unintended slumber. Had been listening to some Jill Scott while monitoring Ivan with the hidden cameras I'd installed in his room at the W. When I dozed off, Ivan was in his boxers standing before the mirror, repeatedly drawing his gun at his reflection like some B-movie gunslinger. Cheesy, overacting, and high. But still functional for what I needed him to do.

Call was from Taralynn.

Surprised me as I'd just seen her. Left her at the dance studio before her fellow dance moms started asking questions. Or got too good of a look at me to where they could remember details beyond "he was black and this tall."

Started not to answer the phone as I looked at the caller ID that read S. SUMMER, the name under which I'd stored the number.

Had moved out of the false spot on Delachaise, so she'd never find me.

All I had to do next was ditch the phone and cut off the throwaway number attached to it.

But what if something happened?

My mind raced back to Bricks's people and the fat one, Ezell. Maybe my job was done for me. But she wouldn't call me if her husband were dead. Or would she?

Best to find out no matter the reason for the call.

Tried to convince myself it was practical logic and not concern for Taralynn as I caught the call just before it went over to voice mail.

“Where are you?” Taralynn asked.

“Huh . . . what?” I responded, still groggy as I sat up in the bed. On the laptop monitor, Ivan was visible in the bathroom this time as he was getting dressed to go out, stopping to admire his abs and check his teeth in the mirror.

“Hold on one second,” I said to Taralynn as I placed her call on mute.

Grabbed another phone off the bedspread and dialed Ivan’s number with it.

“Yo,” he said as I watched him on the monitor. Was almost like Skype. Except he didn’t know he was being watched.

“If you go out tonight, try to do it in moderation. *Capisce?*”

“Yeah, I gotcha, bro.”

“And leave your little friend in the room. I don’t want to hear about you getting popped on Bourbon Street with it.”

“Of course. No worries.”

“And nobody back to the room with you tonight. At least not that room. Remember to scrub it in the morn before you check out.”

“With what this job is paying me, I can accommodate all of that. Now can you stop nagging me?”

I hung up, watching him flipping the bird at the phone on which he’d just spoken.

“Sorry,” I said to Taralynn as I took her off mute. “Thought I heard someone at the door.”

"Where are you?" she repeated, this time irritation apparent in her voice.

"Um . . . at my place. I was sleepin'."

"Bull. I just went by there. By your place on Delachaise."

Shit.

"Said I was asleep. Probably didn't hear you," I said, stifling a fake yawn.

"The elderly woman across the street saw me knocking. She said you didn't live there. That you left. What's really going on, Truth?"

Knew I should've kept the house on Delachaise a few days longer. But needed to be ready to leave quickly and cleanly.

I began to speak. "Well . . . I—"

"Were you evicted?" she asked, cutting me off. It was less a question than it was a declaration of what she knew to be my reality.

My brow furrowed. Then I had to hold back a laugh. "Look . . . I'm just going through some living arrangement issues. Nothing to be worried about," I replied, letting my own mock worry seep and ooze into each statement.

"So where are you? Stop bullshitting me, boy. We go back too far for that."

"Downtown," I answered honestly. "And what's so important?" I asked to shift the conversation away from my living arrangements and to what she really wanted.

"One of the girls turned her ankle and won't be performing in Boston. The instructor found a last-minute replacement, but some of the roles are being switched to accommodate that change. They're working it out now, so going to be another long night. I had a moment to spare and was going stir crazy in there, so . . ."

"So you wanted to talk some more? Gosh, ma'am. Never thought I was that good a conversationalist," I playfully jabbed. Wanted Taralynn, as a grown-ass woman of means, to come clean about her undue concern for me.

"Don't sell yourself short. Your conversation is just what I need. It was crazy luck running into you, Truth. I've learned to savor special moments and these few with you . . . have been good," she admitted. Can't say I wasn't pleased. "Where are you? If you're out on the street, I'll come and get you. Please. Let me do this."

"Okay. Fine," I let up. "But I'm not 'on the street.' I'm at the Holiday Inn on Loyola. Stopped here just to get off my feet . . . while I try to figure things out. They were nice enough to let me chill on a couch in the lobby as long as I minded my own business and didn't bother the guests," I said as I rolled my eyes at my own bullshit.

"Sit tight. I just turned on St. Charles. I'll be right there. Will call when I arrive."

After hanging up. I hurriedly put back on the clothes I was wearing when I stopped by the dance academy. Took the elevator downstairs with a backpack filled with just the innocuous stuff I was able to cram inside—a few sets of clothes, toiletries, and my laptop.

True to my lie, I found an unoccupied sofa in the lobby and took a seat, making my impromptu home in time for Taralynn's call.

But rather than calling, she walked in. I guess she needed to see it for herself.

"You surprised me. Thought you were going to call," I said, pretending not to see her until the last minute. She stood there, already statuesque in height, arms folded.

"Found a parking spot," she acknowledged.

"If you want to hang out before you go back, we could just sit here," I said as I shifted my carefully placed stuff around on the sofa to accommodate her.

"And then where are you going to go?" she asked, still not moving. "They're not going to let you camp out all night, no matter how fine you look."

"Fine," I repeated with a nervous laugh. "I'd take *stable* over fine right about now."

Taralynn looked at her watch again. "Wait here," she said with a devilish smile.

As I rearranged things in my backpack, Taralynn sauntered over to the hotel's front desk. Saw her discuss something as I feared she was asking them about my situation. Just my luck that they'd tell her I was a paying customer who had a room. Then I'd have to come up with something again to cover myself.

She talked with the staff person a moment longer before opening her purse and pulling out cash. Thought she was paying him for information before she returned with a room key.

"What are you doing?" I asked.

"What does it look like, Truth?" she asked as she held the key out for me to take. "It's the key to your room," she said.

Busted.

27

"What do you mean my room?" I asked. I'd gotten too cute with my plotting. Now she knew I was lying about being out on the street. Should've never let her meet me here.

But I wanted to see her.

"Just what I said. It's your room, silly. Told you I'd help you out. Just got you a king guestroom for two weeks."

"Oh," I uttered, a smile of relief that my paranoia and nerves were wrong. But saw Taralynn had paid cash. She didn't want to leave a credit card trail of any sort. It felt like something other than just helping out a friend. "Thanks, but I wasn't asking you to do this," I said as I perused the key card she'd handed me. The room was on the same floor as mine, but three doors down.

"I know. I called you," she said smartly. She still wouldn't join me on the sofa. Just stood there like I was insulting her or something.

"I'm guessing you don't want to talk down here," I mumbled, finally getting it.

"You'd be guessing right," she replied. "Don't need any scandals . . . real or trumped up. You know how this town can be."

"Say no more," I joked as I got off my ass and walked with her to the elevator.

We rode up to the eighth floor. Deadly silent as we passed a room for which a corresponding key sat at the bottom of my backpack. As I placed the key in the slot to my new room courtesy of Taralynn, she pressed up against me, her hand caressing my arm.

I didn't stop or discourage her.

I was letting myself get lost in a different time when two crazy kids acted up over a decade ago. Except this time, instead of saving her future afterward, I would be shattering it.

A sole lamp illuminated the room. I went to turn on the main light switch, but she stopped me.

"You sure about this?" I asked before proceeding farther into the room. There was still time for the adults to win out.

"After you left, the other ladies were talking about how fine you were. Wondering how you might be," Taralynn's darkened, tempting form uttered. Could make out a grin. "They said I was behaving more like you were a long-lost lover than my cousin."

"What did you tell them?"

"I said they were crazy . . . and horny."

"And what are you?"

"Crazy . . . horny," the DA's wife whispered in my ear, her warm breath assaulting my senses. "What are you feeling?" she asked, a hand brushing against my thigh. Daring to come closer than that.

"That you're trying to buy me. Take advantage of my misfortune for a good time," I said as the room door closed completely. The room seemed darker. Like reason was retreating with the light.

"For a good time? Yes, I'd like that. Would like that very much," she said as she dropped her purse. "But I don't have much time. I want to feel like your Summer again. Feel what she felt that time on the lake back then. Am I wrong for that, Truth?"

I responded, taking her in my arms and pulling her closer. She gasped as I kissed her down her neck and across her exposed shoulder, biting at it. Her perfume was freshly applied. Alien by Thierry Mugler assaulted my senses as I imagined her in her Mercedes placing it strategically before entering the hotel. The wicked notion drove me crazy; made me want her even more.

Taralynn unbuttoned my shirt, hastily yanking at the last few buttons to get it off me. She kissed my chest, sucking on my nipples as she grasped my shoulders. She had to feel my hard-on through my pants.

But as I cupped her ass, I paused. "I don't have any condoms on me," I admitted. So much for being prepared for anything. "Wasn't expecting this. But I can run downstairs . . ."

"No time. I don't want you . . . to leave me," she hissed as she placed a finger to my lips and nipped at my neck. "But we can still . . . do other things," she offered as she removed the ankle boots which almost brought her to my height.

"Okay," I agreed, smiling.

I grasped her tunic and pulled it over her head, watching her shaking her hair loose. We kissed again, our tongues feverishly working as I reached around and undid her bra. A bit of modesty crept in from the married woman, Taralynn shielding her breasts from my sight with her hands. I gently moved her hands aside, sucking and caressing each lovely mound as I reached into her jeans. She responded. Undid the buttons on her jeans and stepping out of them one gorgeous long leg at a time. As she stood before me, I could make out the tiny lace trim outline along the top of her thong. A faint piece of fabric highlighting what I'm sure was still a gorgeous pussy.

Beautiful. Vulnerable. Wanting.

"I want to taste you," I grunted. Watched strong legs tremble with anticipation.

I scooped her up and carried her to the unspoiled bed where I slid off her thong. Lowered myself atop her, starting at her lips, kissing of them succulently to start off my journey down her body. Taralynn's hands rested atop my head, guiding me over her breasts and down her perfumed stomach.

"Uh huh. Uh huh," she called out as she felt my breath on her neatly trimmed strip of pubic hairs. Fingers that were along for the ride, gently guiding me before, now gripped my scalp and nuzzled my head between her legs. I inhaled deeply of her natural essence as I plunged my face, my tongue sampling her at first and finding her oh so wet.

I ate her out good, sucking and lapping at her clit while sliding two fingers in and out of her pussy, fucking her with them as I took my thumb and toyed with her asshole. Brought Taralynn to tears on the bed as I camped out between her legs, pleasuring her to climax after climax until my neck began to cramp.

Pushed beyond her limits, Taralynn had me roll onto my back.

"Give it," she said, motioning toward my dick as she climbed atop my face, smothering me with her delightful pussy as she leaned over and took me in her mouth.

She gripped my dick tightly, clenching it in one hand while caressing my balls with the other. Listened to her humming with each bob of her head, lips sealed just right. Felt shivers as she sucked me like she was trying to draw venom from out of a wound. Then she went sloppy, slurping and gulping on my head, causing me to lose my mind.

I grabbed her ass cheeks, spreading them wide and keeping her pussy situated like so as I tasted and licked every drop of her goodness that dare escape. As she came, her quivering and quaking hips involuntarily drove her even harder against my lips, which were kissing her with an abandon reserved for lovers.

"Ooooh, ooooh. Shit. Fuck. Damn. Oooooh, fawk," she moaned and cursed, trying to catch her breath as the sixty-nine overwhelmed her. Then she redoubled her efforts on my dick, not one for falling short on her end of our erotic equation tonight.

"Mmm hmm. Let it go. Let it all go," she demanded as she felt the twitches and shuddering in my pelvis, a storm gathering inside that she'd summoned. As my eruption built up beyond my control, I sucked even harder on her clit. Trying to kill and resuscitate her pussy in the same breath.

"I . . . I . . ." I stuttered.

Then I felt it in my toes.

The tiny warning before my load exploded forth, slamming inside Taralynn's mouth. She swallowed it all, sucking me dry and lapping at the remaining cum on my head.

"Oh . . . oh my gawd," she sputtered, rolling off me. Coughing as she tried to catch her breath.

I lay there, totally spent as well. Watching her chest rise and fall in the dark.

And wondering why.

Despite this opportunity presenting itself for recklessness, she didn't come searching for me just to fuck.

But I decided not to dwell on it. Any more talk might lead unexpected destinations.

Just keep it physical.

Same as where I left it thirteen years ago.

Then she had to leave. Watch she left on her wrist reminding her of duties beyond her most primal pleasure.

She said nothing other than to gather her clothes and go in the bathroom to tidy up, wearily dragging herself out several minutes later and kissing me on the cheek. Told me stay put and to not go downstairs with her lest someone see us together.

I had a vested interest in not being seen with her either, so I remained.

Remained in the room paid for by the woman whose husband I had to kill tomorrow.

But tonight?

Tonight, I would just sleep.

28

Should've slept soundly after Taralynn left.

Especially after what we'd done.

Instead I dreamed.

Risk associated with coming back to New Orleans.

More of those dreams.

Dreams like that.

Dreams of my mom.

Of a day after we'd moved here from California.

Pre-Katrina times.

Settled in courtesy of my Uncle Jason.

"Momma?" I calmly called to the woman staring out the window at the large oak tree. Waited for Leila Marie North to reply.

Nothing.

She hadn't spoken in days and was barely eating.

Only the gumbo from Dooky Chase. And that was when she felt like it.

"Truth!" Uncle Jason yelled. Was waiting on me. But I ran back here to check on my mom because she needed me more.

"Momma," I called out again, a little more urgently this time. Used to be Mommy when we were in California. Didn't feel right here. Mommy felt soft. I had to be hard now. That's what my Uncle Jason told me. "Do you want me to get you something?" I asked, pleading as I walked up to the window sill next to her and took her hand.

She didn't answer. Instead, tears began streaming down her face as she broke into a smile. I didn't know what it meant, but it scared me.

"Boy, didn't you hear me calling you?" Jason called out as he appeared in the doorway, looking at the two of us. Those eyes of his looked irritated despite the goatee-lined smile he flashed. Over these years, I was learning that his face rarely matched what was going on in his head.

"Yeah, but, my momma—"

"Is also my sister, dear boy," he said, curtly cutting me off. "And I know how best to deal with this."

"Yessir," I responded. "But I think she needs help."

"And she'll get it, Truth," he said as he entered the room and placed his hand on her back. "I promise you. But for now we have to get going. Flight waiting to take us to Atlanta. I have some talent evaluations with which you can help me. You ever been to Atlanta?"

"No, sir."

"Well, you're in for a treat. Once we've wrapped up, might even take you by a place called Magic City."

Place sounded nice. Reminded me of Disney and "the Magic Kingdom." Leila Marie was supposed to take me to Disneyland when we were in California. But we only rode past it once in a taxi cab. She said it was due to her busy work schedule and planning her wedding to Randall Fischer from *Promises for Tomorrow,* but one day we'd get there.

"Can we get her some gumbo from Dooky Chase before we leave?"

"I'll have one of my people pick it up."

"She likes the one with okra," I reminded him, concerned his people wouldn't get it right.

Checking his watch as it slid free from beneath his sport coat sleeve, he said, "Told you I got it now c'mon. We have places to go and people to see. Leave her. She'll be fine, dear boy. She'll be fine."

As I backed away and let go of my mom's hand, she turned my way. Left that damn tree outside her window alone momentarily. "I'm sorry," she said to me. Voice was different. Like butterflies and sunshine. Like it used to be when she was happy and in love.

Had almost forgotten that sound.

I just nodded and smiled.

Left for the airport where we flew out to Atlanta with Jason North and some of his other On-Phire people.

As far as my mom, she wasn't there when I came back as a man, having lost my virginity at Magic City even though I was too young to be on the premises.

Leila Marie North was nowhere that I would ever be capable of reaching.

Ever.

She jumped that day.

Off the Mississippi River Bridge, the older span of the Crescent City Connection.

A few days later, her body was fished from the water downriver in St. Bernard Parish.

The *Times-Picayune* would report on the failed soap star who plunged to her death. And who left no children behind. With no birth certificate and never having attended school, I didn't exist to the world.

And Jason kept it that way.

For he would be my teacher.

And I would be his star pupil.

I woke up, sitting upright in a cold, hard sweat. Cleared my head then checked the time.

Had been asleep for hours.

I packed up my stuff, removing all traces of my DNA from the room and stormed three doors down to my actual room. Was calling Ivan before I even inserted my key in the door.

"Ain't you up kinda early?" Ivan asked upon answering. Could hear the sounds of laughter and music in the background.

"No. I don't sleep," I replied, wishing it were the truth. "You ready to go over this again?"

The sooner I left New Orleans the better.

29

"Status?" Mr. Smith asked.

"Today," I replied calmly as I peered through a set of tiny binoculars at a residence down the block. "And we are through."

"Absolutely," he said, not realizing that it wasn't a question.

"Well let me do my job so we never speak again," I replied as I hung up.

The grass in which I was laying was still damp. Had been concealed here for hours. Since before the sprinklers came on at dawn. Fearing a random dog giving me away despite my camouflage. All this fucked-up and impromptu planning coming to this moment.

Outside the Roy residence, watching and waiting.

And waiting some more.

Could've planted a camera and monitored remotely. Or paid someone to be out here at English Turn instead. But this had become personal. Beyond just protecting Collette in Texas or my own hide. I needed to see this through to its inevitable conclusion.

Ensure nothing went wrong.

Two standard NOPD cruisers came on shift in front of the home, replacing the other two that were here when I slinked into position. Fresh off my night with the DA's wife.

Everything depended on Rodney Roy being true to his nature—the driven professional. Then shaping that to my ends.

So I continued to wait for him to leave his house. Hoping that he would and soon. Before the neighborhood woke up and I might be exposed.

From beneath my cover, consisting of a tarp and some netting, I was checking my other phones when a noise got my attention. Was the sound of a car door slamming shut, which carried through the stillness of the morn. I peered out, raising my binoculars and taking a look. One of the NOPD officers outside Roy's house had exited his car. Could see him on his radio with someone. Then, as if on cue, the garage door rose up. A silver Cadillac CTS began slowly backing out. I zoomed in for a closer look, catching the passenger window as it dropped for the DA to talk to the officer. He was alone.

Good.

Rather than trying to read his lips, I checked my watch before me and turned on the mini police scanner on my belt, popping an earpiece in place. Timing was critical. Tiny windows of opportunity in which I had to operate. I picked up one of my phones and sent a simple text. To anyone but the person for whom it was intended, it would seem like an innocent message rather than what it really was—a "go" code.

To get the DA heading down the right rabbit hole, I had to control traffic. The first text was the prompt, setting up a bad wreck on General DeGaulle Drive to slow him down. Before the DA and his escort were beyond the gates of English Turn, my scanner alerted me that phase one was a success. I yanked the battery and SIM card from the phone I'd just used. Grasped another phone as it was time for another text.

This one was a little more risky. An overturned tanker truck on the Crescent City Connection to bring traffic crossing to the East Bank to a screeching halt. Determined to get to work, that would leave the DA with one surefire route.

The Algiers Ferry where Ivan would be waiting.

But before I pushed the button to send the second "go" code, something stilled my hand. Thoughts of that damned bridge. Visions of my mom for the final time still lingering from my dreams. And her saying she was sorry to me. Always thought she was saying she was sorry for what she was about to do, leave me. But maybe she was saying she was sorry for what she knew I'd become.

My watch was telling me to shake it off. Not much time left before I had to send the text. Otherwise the DA would get stuck in traffic past the toll plaza and unable to detour to the ferry.

But if I didn't do this, Collette would pay for it with her life.

Time was ticking.

I moved my thumb to send the second text when my personal phone buzzed. From beneath my cover, I paused as an early morning jogger stopped to check her pulse rate. Once she resumed her run, unaware I was less than ten feet away, I turned to the incoming call.

It was Taralynn.

Tick tock as Mr. Smith had said.

Shouldn't have answered it, but . . .

"Hello?" I said trying to appear normal.

"Hey. It's me. You still asleep?" Taralynn asked softly.

"No. Just out for some coffee," I replied, voice still low from my spot. "You getting ready for your big trip to Boston?"

"Yeah. Doing some packing for me and Sasha. Couldn't sleep very well once I came home last night," she uttered, acknowledging what had happened between us. "Figured I'd get up since my husband was going in to the office."

"On a Sunday? He's not spending the day with you guys before you leave?" I asked, feigning surprise and disgust.

"Work calls. Duty to the public and all," she mumbled, not sounding too convincing. Could hear her fumbling around what probably was their kitchen. Imagined her in a house coat, fixing a cup of coffee or preparing breakfast for her daughter before they attended church or something. Family stuff.

Just then I looked down and sent the text for the second accident. It was time to get out of here and let the rest of this play out.

"Well," was my only comment.

"Truth, I . . . I know it's inappropriate. Even after last night. But I was kinda wondering if I could see you before our flight."

"That might be hard to do," I replied, checking my watch again and calculating in my head where things should be about now. Time to leave New Orleans and not look back. That included Taralynn. "It was good seeing you again after all this time. It's been fun, but I don't feel right about how things went down. Going to repay you for the money you spent on the hotel room as soon as I can, by the way."

"The money's no problem. Just helping out like I said. And I don't want you to think I was paying for your services. It wasn't that kind of thing. I really hope you don't feel that way about me, Truth," she offered, trying to salvage whatever she thought this was.

Poor thing.

"Uh . . . Don't know how to tell you, but I'm leaving town. Got some work lined up for me, so. . . ." I said, letting my voice trail off.

"So that's it?" she asked, her voice raising an octave. Good-byes were never easy.

"Yeah. That's it. Like I said, I don't feel right about what went down. You're a married woman. And I'm not the home wrecker type. So, it's probably best that we say good-bye now, Summer."

"Truth, Sasha's not Rodney's daughter," she blurted out.

"Oh?" I voiced, wondering if she was insinuating that their home life wasn't as perfect as made out to be.

"She's his stepdaughter."

"Okay. But he still loves her . . . and you, right?" I pushed, trying to get through this without hurting her anymore. There was no chance for us.

"Yes, Truth. But that's not what I'm trying to say. Will you just listen!" Taralynn shouted to assert herself, startling me.

"Okay. I'm listening," I said as I sprang to my feet, rolling up the tarp and netting I'd used for concealment and quickly backing out of the sightline of her house.

"When I said Sasha was nine, I lied. She's twelve, Truth."

"What are you saying?" I asked, my body suddenly feeling like I'd been Tasered. My mind filled with things other than the plan on which I needed to be focused.

Thought the girl was just tall for her age because of her mother's height, but now . . .

The math. The math.

"She's your daughter, Truth. Sasha's your daughter."

30

"Truth? Are you there?" Taralynn called out as I stood exposed in the open on her neighbor's lawn. In the other ear, my police scanner was squawking about the major traffic snarl on the Crescent City Connection. But my head rang like someone had just smacked me with a hammer.

"Yeah," I replied, the ringing still there.

"Did you hear me? I said Sasha's your daughter," she repeated.

"You said she was nine. You . . . lied," I recited, anger welling up inside.

"I know. I already said I lied. What was I supposed to do? You just showed up! I was stunned! I . . . I wanted to tell you. Last night, but . . ."

"But we . . . only once," I said, fumbling for words.

"Yes. And I got pregnant."

Mine.

All this time and I never knew.

I was a . . . father.

But I was about to take away the only father Sasha knew.

As in mythology as in life, the fates were cruel.

"I have to go. Need to digest everything. I . . . I'll call you back. And then we'll talk some more about this. I promise," I said, having not yet determined if I was telling the truth. All I knew was that I had to stop that which I'd set in motion, no matter the consequences.

I ran down English Turn Drive heading west toward East Canal Street where I had a bogus neighborhood security van parked on the corner with East Sixth Street. One mile that felt like ten. Had been dialing Ivan's phone relentlessly, each time getting the voice mail that hadn't been set up.

"Bro, what are you doing calling?" Ivan asked as he finally responded.

"I'm calling it off. Abort the mission," I replied, slowing down enough to be understood.

"*Abort the mission?*" Ivan repeated mockingly. "This ain't no Tom Clancy, nigga."

"Let it go, man. Change in plans. Going to revisit another day," I said, trying a different tact with the cokehead. Make that *armed and dangerous cokehead.*

"Nah. Nah. I'm gonna do my fuckin' job. And then you're gonna pay me my motherfuckin' money!"

"You do this there won't be any fuckin' money," I stressed as I arrived at the van, chest hurting and trying to catch my breath.

I was a father.

"And I'm sayin' fuck you. Those Russians from prison you were joking about? The ones that kept me alive? Well, I owe them. Big. Told them they'd have their money next week. So I'm gonna cap this motherfucker and then you're gonna pay me my motherfuckin' money. And then I'm goin' back to Cali and fuck Sophia. I ain't your bitch, bitch," he said, hanging up.

"Fuck!" I yelled at the top of my lungs, swinging wildly at the air in frustration. My phone flew out my hand, breaking against the van's windshield before I could stop it.

Left a multi-splintered crack across my field of vision.

Allowed myself the briefest of seconds to stare at the shattered spider web in the glass before I started the van and sped away.

31

I sped down General Meyer Avenue like I stole something, running the red light at the intersection with Shirley Drive right in front of the former Naval Support Activity facility. An old Ford LTD clipped me as I passed, but I held the van on the road and kept going. Ignored the horns honking and the car in my rearview mirror trying to get my license plate number. When the avenue flowed into the two-lane Newton Street, I knew I was getting closer to Algiers Point and the ferry. Figured I'd made up some time on the DA and his escort. I went a few more blocks then turned right onto Elmira Avenue, speeding even faster on the dangerously thin street.

At the corner with Patterson Drive, I conveniently came upon a bus lot for Orleans Parish Schools on my left. Without braking, I swerved into the open grass lot and stowed the van between two large yellow-orange monsters. Changed my shoes and shirt in the back then made my way to the levee along the Mississippi River where I ran the half mile toward Morgan Street and the Algiers Ferry Landing.

Emerging from behind the Algiers Point Condominiums, I descended the sloping grass-covered levee into the area parking lot. And right next to it, on Morgan Street, was the line of cars, trucks, and SUVs waiting on the ferry. Vehicle traffic was heavier than I anticipated. A testament no doubt to how bad I'd fucked shit up on the bridge.

Started this morning with a risky plan that now I had to dismantle. But if the DA's car had already crossed, I would've preferred it. Other than a report of my hit and run on General Meyer, there was no mention of anything else on the scanner I was still using to eavesdrop, so maybe Ivan got cold feet. Punk ass wasn't a natural killer anyway, but that was why I picked him to carry it out. An expendable fool whose influence Sophia would be free of once this was over.

Now, after striking the match, I held it too long. Was too close to the fire. Torn between competing interests, all of them surrounding women. Sophia, who was so much like me, but whom I never could love for that very same reason. Collette, who I loved with all my twisted heart, but who I could never have because she loathed the true me. And now Taralynn, wife of my target, but also the mother of my child.

After another quick glance at my watch, I saw the ferry was nearing its departure time. Removing my earpiece, I dropped the scanner into my backpack and pulled out my Saints baseball cap, donning it for any surveillance cameras that would be picking me up. I sped up my pace, still looking for the DA's Cadillac and its police escort among traffic waiting to board.

They weren't there.

So I knew what I had to do.

Enter a ferry to confront an armed man on the river where my mother took her life. With no weapons and no means of escape.

But I had an advantage over him. My mind.

That and Ivan only knowing his part of the plan.

For there was always more.

Smiling at the challenge, I entered the landing with the rest of the pedestrians.

As the ferry pulled away from the landing, knew I had less than twenty minutes to figure it all out, to locate Ivan and the DA. With the way the cars were loaded, wasn't hard to spot the lights atop the police car. Looked like only one made the trip across with him. Maybe the other was called into service with the wreck on the bridge. Still hadn't spotted Ivan yet, so I quickly made my way past the other passengers and into the restroom where his change of clothes was placed. Found the bag tucked behind a garbage can and peered inside. Clothes reeking of alcohol and sweat from Ivan's partying were crammed on top. Beneath them was the untouched NOPD uniform. Confirmed what I feared. He was on the boat and committed to going through with this. I removed Ivan's clothes and hastily dumped them in the garbage can. Made the bag more compact, allowing me to store it inside my backpack, which I then stashed behind a ventilation grille before anybody came in.

Grabbed a tourist brochure then set about finding Ivan. Noticed the DA first as two NOPD officers were positioned near his car while he stayed inside on a phone call of some sort. Maybe he was telling his wife and daughter how much he loved them.

I unfolded my guide, playing the tourist as I strolled along the safety rail. Admiring the skyline of downtown New Orleans with the Aquarium of the Americas and the Riverwalk and the eastern edge of the Vieux Carré, with St. Louis Cathedral, from the water. On the upper deck next to the ferry wheelhouse, one of the workers leaned on the railing while he surveyed the assorted human cargo as well. Didn't allow it to hold my attention for too long as we both had jobs to do.

Then I spotted Ivan by his walk and uniform that didn't match perfectly with the rest of the crew. Was on approach from the other end of the ferry where he'd probably been checking for the Cadillac he'd just found. Had let him get too close to the DA, but he knew a signal awaited for him to do his job, which was to walk up and plant a bullet into Rodney Roy. That and the NOPD officer hovering near the DA's car door were the only things that kept him at bay. From beneath his crewman's hat, he checked his flashy watch, which didn't fit his attire. The clock inside my head spurred me into action.

Tourist guide in hand, I eased along the rail. His hand was resting inside the jacket, glazed-over eyes locked in with a sole purpose, so he wasn't paying attention to this lone tourist. Noticing where we were on the river cover, I spoke.

"Excuse me, sir. Can you tell me where the French Market is on this map?" I asked as I placed my tourist guide between him and his view of the DA. Irritated, he quickly turned toward me, his eyes overcome with recognition and surprise.

"Bro, you need to step the fuck off," he hissed, probably thinking it was a whisper in his deluded state.

"Put it away, man. Just calm down and wait for the ferry to dock," I said, smiling for the other passengers as I now placed myself between Ivan and the DA, pretending like I was having a friendly conversation. "You don't want to do this anyway."

"Get the fuck out my way, bro," he said as he glanced around me at the Cadillac. Rodney had lowered his window to take in the sea breeze just then, making it even easier for Ivan to get a clean shot off.

"What? If you kill me you wouldn't get your money anyway. But I got a newsflash for you. There's no money."

"What do you mean there's no money?"

"This isn't a paying job, bro," I said, mimicking him with the annoyance. "The money I've been giving you is mine. You're just a mark. Welcome to the real game, Ivan," I taunted at the precise moment the Algiers Ferry reached the halfway point on the river.

At that opportune moment, from the opposite side of the ferry, Ivan's signal came.

"Oh my God! Somebody's overboard!" a woman screamed at the top of her lungs while hysterically waving and pointing down at the water. Ferry passengers, including the DA's police detail, scrambled in the direction of her frantic pleas, not knowing that it was a baby doll that had been dropped by the woman. Then with the distraction, when Ivan was supposed to walk up and do his job, I rushed him. Held him up for a second during his confusion while still flapping my map around as if in a sudden, frightening tussle.

"What the fuck!" Ivan exclaimed as he tried to push me off. I suddenly released my grip on his wrist allowing his handgun to come free as I spun around and retreated.

Give him the briefest of smiles as he stood with his weapon exposed.

Right as I turned and fell overboard.

As if knocked aside by Ivan.

Savored his clueless stare. But the ferry worker watching from above, the one I'd paid to simply point out Ivan to the police at that precise moment, did his job despite the sudden change I'd introduced.

"He's got a gun!" I heard him yell as gravity took hold of my body. Gunshots rang out on the deck of the ferry just as the Mighty Mississippi took me in its violent embrace.

By getting on the ferry, I'd inserted myself into the equation.

Now, as darkness claimed me, I'd removed myself. All was free to play out the same, except for the final outcome. Rodney Roy would live.

Sasha would have a dad.

Her dad.

Felt myself quickly fading as the current and the churning of the ferry's engines overwhelmed and bounced me around like a rag doll. The irony wasn't lost on me that I was going to leave in the same manner as Leila Marie.

Then through the deafening roar and blackness, I felt a pair of hands on me, a hallucination as my oxygen-starved lungs succumbed to the assault. Or that I was finally being dragged down to whatever hell awaited me for my sins.

A brilliant flash of light was my last memory.

Then searing agony and surprise as my eyes adjusted to clouds overhead.

If there was a heaven, I couldn't be there.

"He's alive!" one of the people standing over me yelled to others. I was on the deck of the ferry.

"Sir, are you okay?" a soaked gentleman asked as he leaned too close to my face for comfort. I blinked a few times, comforted by the oxygen entering my lungs. He was NOPD. One of the DA's security detail. I turned my head to the side. Coughed again as I saw a smaller group standing over another body. But that one wasn't moving.

Ivan.

Original plan was for Ivan to kill the DA then for the ferry worker to point him out right as he did it. By stalling Ivan just long enough, I'd succeeded in modifying it.

And somehow I was still . . . alive.

"Sir, are you okay? Do you understand what I'm saying," the officer asked again as he saw my dopey smile. He must've been the one to shoot Ivan then jump overboard to rescue me. A real black Superman he was.

"A man . . . worked for the ferry. He shoved me overboard," I said gasping as I coughed up some more river water from my lungs. "He . . . he had a gun."

"*Had,*" the other officer proudly affirmed, coming into my blurry line of sight as I tried to sit up with assistance. "We got him."

The ferry had stopped dead on the water until I was rescued and revived, but was now getting back underway toward the East Bank. I was unsteadily to my feet, avoiding the DA who'd been moved securely to the ferry's wheelhouse. Crime scene tape had been retrieved from the NOPD cruiser and was being strung up around Ivan's body, which rested in a pool of blood. He got off one shot, not hitting a thing, before they unloaded on him.

"Sir, we're going to have some questions for you when we dock. Just wanted to let you know," my savior said as I stared at Ivan's open eyes. From my silence, the officer probably thought I was traumatized by it all.

"I . . . I feel sick," I mumbled, hands trembling for effect. "Can I use the restroom?"

"I don't see why not. Not like you can go anywhere," he joked.

As I hurried to the bathroom, I could hear the ferry engines beginning to reverse. We were slowing to dock. Thought I had a broken rib, so another jump into the water was out of the question. Rushing inside in my wet clothes, I retrieved my backpack then entered an open stall. Having been for Ivan, the NOPD uniform wasn't a perfect fit for me, but it would do for the short term. Rather than leaving my wet clothes behind, I stuffed them into my backpack after removing a fake moustache that I applied to my face in the restroom in the mirror.

Then I took a deep breath, psyching myself up for one more dangerous round. Placed my hand against the restroom wall as I felt for the engine vibrations. When they came to a halt, I flew out the door. Tried to walk as steady and confident as possible toward the front of the ferry. Instructed the passengers, eager to depart, that they needed to stay put until NOPD had control of the area.

As the boarding ramp dropped and the gates on the East Bank opened, a group of NOPD officers and crime scene investigators were waiting. I walked toward them, hoping they didn't pick up on some of my uniform accoutrements being off or missing.

"What we got? Somebody tried to shoot the DA?"

"Looks like it. Shit was crazy. Jackson got the perp then rescued one of the passengers from the water," I volunteered, remembering my savior's name off his uniform. "Shell casings accounted for and waiting for processing by you guys," I muttered, trying to sound like I knew what I was talking about. "I gotta get another transport for the DA. Don't let any of the passengers and crew off."

Sufficient in my explanation and instructions, they got to work.

And with that performance, I walked past my last impediment to freedom, veering away from the reporters who'd just begun to gather. Water dripping from the backpack I carried as I vanished yet again.

32

"Honey, are you okay? Where's Sasha?" Rodney asked his wife as he entered their home through the front door. She ran into his arms, kissing him. Relief evident.

The opposite of what she was feeling toward me at the moment.

Especially as I showed up inside her house, insisting that she call her husband home without answering any of her questions.

Scared the hell out of Sasha as she was the first one to discover the strange man. Taralynn sent her to her room. Told her to stay there and not come out. It was ever so brief, but I looked at the young girl differently than I had at the dance studio. Wanted to assuage her fears. Tell her it was going to be all right and that I wasn't a bad man.

But children can see through lies.

I sat in a wingback chair in the foyer, silently observing Rodney and Taralynn while careful not to make a sudden move due to my ribs. Wore a dark blue business suit now. A shade similar to his, but minus the gray pinstripes.

"Who the hell are you? And what are you doing in my house?" he asked, protectively stepping in front of his wife when he realized I'd been sitting there.

If this didn't go just right, Rodney's security detail outside the house would be in here and all over me. And in my state, I'd be helpless to do anything about it. Body felt like one big bruise from hitting the water.

"Rodney, wait," Taralynn said as she attempted to calm him. Even though she no longer trusted me. "This gentleman says he's here to help you."

Made Taralynn swear not to use my real name.

Or reveal the extent of our relationship.

In exchange, I conceded certain things.

Things a father shouldn't ever have to concede, but for the greater good.

"Well, you need to start talking now. Because I just survived an attempt on my life, so I have a short fuse."

"I work for an agency that's been monitoring your situation down here in New Orleans. Particularly, your upcoming Braxton Lewis trial," I offered, straining to stand without grimacing.

"What are you? FBI? DEA?" he questioned. Still odd meeting him face-to-face.

"I'd prefer not to divulge those details. But let's just say, things took a severe turn this afternoon."

"So—*pardon my French*—what the fuck does that mean? You boys want me to drop my case? Because I'll be damned if I'm going to let Bricks back on these streets!"

"No. But if you were out of the way, we're pretty sure that there are others in your office prepared to blow the case against this man. On some technicality, if I had to guess. Bricks has money. A lot. And that buys influence," I submitted. Wasn't positive about his coworkers being prepared to bungle the case in his absence, but I was pretty sure. Otherwise Mr. Smith wouldn't be so certain that removing Rodney would resolve his *family matters* problem.

"Before we go any further, show me some ID," he demanded, holding out his hand.

"Can't do that. And if I did, it wouldn't be real," I responded. If I'd had the time, I would've made an ID, but this was all impromptu. A wild attempt to keep him alive and to give me more time.

"And why should I believe you?" he asked, the attorney in him still razor sharp.

"Because I'm here risking my career by going outside the normal channels, Mr. Roy. And because your wife and kid are still safe," I threw out there.

Taralynn looked at me. Still not believing what I was saying. But this really hurt. Ignoring her pain, I pressed on with my lie. Between what I'd learned from Mr. Smith and on my own, I had enough to pull it off. I think.

"What about my wife and kid?" Rodney pushed, getting in my face as Taralynn tugged on his arm.

"We've been watching them. Know that Braxton Lewis's people have been trying to get threats across to you through them. Threats that we've intercepted and neutralized."

Rage flashed in Taralynn's eyes. Eyes I was avoiding as I stared down her husband. She now knew for certain that our meeting was no mere coincidence.

"So what do you want?" he asked, resignation surfacing in his voice for the first time.

"We want you to disappear for forty-eight hours. Seventy-two, if you can afford it. Let folks think that maybe you're incapacitated after what happened on the ferry. If rumors float that you're dead, even better. Go to Boston with your wife and kid. I'm sure they'd like that. Give us time to work out Mr. Lewis's outstanding issues with the Mexican cartels. Then you can continue with your trial. And nail the bastard," I said. I'd saved his life, now had to use him.

"Why should I do this?" he asked, arms folded.

"Because I'm trying to save your life," I replied, careful with the tense. "Something I just shared with Mrs. Roy before you arrived. Go, Mr. Roy. Go to Boston with your wife and kid. Be a husband . . . and a father to them. I'm not asking you to do any more than that. No compromise to your integrity. I promise."

The DA paced for a moment, digesting my words. Looked at his wife then me. This morning there'd been a bullet with his name on it.

"What's it going to be, Mr. DA?" I asked.

The Mercedes GLK came to a stop outside a home in Pontchartrain Park, one of the first subdivisions developed by and for middle-class African Americans in the city. Taralynn released the hatch and I rolled out onto my feet, wobbly from overexertion and my ordeal on the ferry. As I straightened my suit, saw the block was over halfway back after the floodwaters of Katrina had inundated the neighborhood. I walked around and joined her inside the SUV.

"Who's house?" I asked.

"My parents' . . . well, my father's. Only place Rodney would let me go when I offered to get you out of the house and past the police."

"Thank you."

"For what, Truth?" she scoffed. "I don't know you. I mean . . . I *really* don't know you. Can't tell what's a lie and what's the—*no pun intended*—truth anymore. I . . . I thought you were down on your luck, but obviously you're not. I thought that maybe you had some lingering feelings for me, but obviously you don't. And the things I . . . I did with you. That I wanted to do with you. Now you claim to work for the government . . . and it all sounds convincing. Since I've been so far in the dark, did you know Sasha was yours before I told you?"

"No. Honestly."

"So your being surprised was real?"

"Yes. Totally. Still trying to process it. I had no idea. I swear. Wouldn't have left you in a situation like that," I replied, wanting to reach out and take her hand. But thinking better of it.

Taralynn sighed then shook her head. Checked her phone as Rodney was expecting her call. "What's really going on, Truth?" she asked. Disappointment and frustration permeated her every word.

"I owe you that at least. Because of our history. And as the mother of my child," I mouthed.

"Yes. You do, you asshole."

I stared at her dashboard for a moment. Then turned my gaze upward, looking out the windshield. Lake Pontchartrain wasn't too far away. The place where Sasha was conceived over a decade ago. "Someone wants your husband dead," I began, taking that first dangerous step. "Because of the trial. That someone blackmailed me. I was supposed to have Rodney killed. I didn't."

"You . . . Were you on the ferry today? With Rodney?" Taralynn inquired, aghast at the idea as the words escaped her mouth. She clenched the steering wheel, her hands trembling.

I simply nodded.

"And the people who blackmailed you? What about them?"

"I'll deal with it," I answered. "The less you know the better. Just get your husband out of town like you promised."

"And you'll stay away from Sasha like you promised?" she stressed.

"Yes."

"Truth?"

"Huh?"

"Did you use me?" she asked with her final question, her voice cracking now as she turned away so I wouldn't see her wipe the tear from her eye.

"Yes, but only as much as you let me," I voiced. "Nothing more."

I took her slap as well as I could, the side of my face stinging.

Now she'd hate me.

And that hate would burn brightly through any delusions she had about our past.

"I won't be responsible for what happens if you ever come around me or my family again," she said as she started the Benz, Summer gone for good. "I need to call my husband. Let him know I made it okay and that you're gone. Now get out."

I complied, realizing that good-byes would've been hollow. Just got out and closed the door behind me. As I walked away, hearing Taralynn's sobs and screams, I left convinced that Sasha not knowing me was for the better.

Sasha had plenty of time to forget the man in the suit who showed up in their house one day, never to be seen again.

Hoped the Roy family's time in Boston would be a good thing for them.

But my immediate thoughts took me to a place on the opposite coast.

Where long-delayed information was needed immediately.

"Got that cell location you promised me?" I asked without so much as a greeting for the man who was supposed to be tracking Mr. Smith's original call that time in Portland.

"Yeah, I got it," he replied. "And I'm sorry it took so long, but you gotta keep my name outta this."

"Consider it done. You just focus on your daughter's first day at Stanford. You're lucky to have that relationship with her. Cherish it," I said.

"Thank you," he said as he fumbled with my comments. "So we are done, yes?"

"Yes," I uttered before hanging up.

We were done.

But I was just beginning with Mr. Smith.

33

"Frisco PD. Officer Kane," he answered over the buzz of activity in the background.

"Desk duty already? Can't keep you down, huh?" I joked as I sat cloaked in a hoodie and sunglasses at Five Star Coffee & Espresso in Severn, Maryland, my phone call to Texas having been routed through three different countries. Had just flown into BWI after a brief layover in Miami. No plans on getting a hotel room for this trip. Was running lean for what I was doing.

"It was an undisplaced fracture. Thanks for asking," Officer Kane spat. "Can't drive for a while because of the cast, but I'll take that over being six feet under."

"No respect for the badge these days. Did you get the license plate?" I asked, continuing with the small talk in case his calls were being monitored at the station.

"Course not. Caught me right as I turned my back to get in my car. Then avoided my dash cam. Like it was intentional."

"Imagine that. Crazy people, I tell ya. How's the Mrs.?"

"Good. All good. I'm hoping you called to tell me the streets are safe again for folk," he commented, referring to the outstanding threat on Collette's life by Mr. Smith.

"I'm working hard on cleaning them. Gutters and drains too. Which is why I called."

"The purse?" he asked, referring to the gift I'd left him at our last meeting. The one where he'd drawn his gun on me.

"Actually it's a clutch, but yes," I said, correcting him about the woman's accessory. Had tossed it into his police car as I drove by. Left it wrapped in a plastic bag with a note attached. Note asked Kane to discretely run any prints he might find on the surface, a surface specially prepared so as to register under a black light any hands that might have touched it. Such as the fingers of a flirtatious Mr. Smith at Mickey Mantle's in Oklahoma City. One of the few times he was particularly careless. But I'd handpicked the blonde for that job. Was a dancer for the Oklahoma City Thunder. Told her I was a grad assistant at OU filming a scene for a college film project. She performed her role flawlessly.

"Got a match," Kane said under his breath. "Virginia driver's license. Centreville. Had a DUI two years ago. Is this him?"

"No, but getting closer," I lied. Kane had a mad-on for him, especially after the broken leg, but vengeance was going to be mine. I already knew Mr. Smith frequented the DC-Maryland-Virginia area, or the "DMV" as the locals called it, based on the cell phone tower info I already had. That's why I was out here. Fishing and hoping I'd land the big one. But now, like a guided missile, I had a target lit up like a Christmas tree for me.

Time to go boom.

"Can you e-mail the info?" I asked Kane.

"Yeah. How soon do you need it?"

"Now would be good as I'm kinda on the clock," I stressed, gulping down the last of my cup of coffee as I prepared to head over to Virginia.

***

I hunkered down outside the Whole Foods Market off Fair Lakes Parkway in Fairfax, Virginia. His voice mail to his wife said he was stopping here after work. Of course, he didn't specify which Whole Foods, but I picked the closest one to their home. Watching everyone who entered.

Of course, if he didn't show up, I knew where to find him now. Had been pulling up the driver's license photo from Kane on my phone again and again all afternoon. And moving my car around on the parking lot lest someone monitoring the surveillance cameras at this new location got suspicious.

Wondered if this was how he felt when he stopped a whole plane for me in Chicago. Probably felt pretty smug looking at me on a monitor somewhere while barking out orders to people who had no clue how badly he was abusing his power.

At 3:47 P.M., I got lucky. And someone got unlucky. Watched him enter the store with his cell to his ear. Probably still trying to reach his wife. I got out the Chrysler 300 in a Georgetown T-shirt and sweatpants with non-descript white Nike tennis shoes.

Oh. And a pair of gloves.

Followed my subject inside the bastion of the overly pretentious P.C. and the annoyingly healthy, first to the floral department where he grabbed a batch of fresh roses. Either for his wife or another mistress. Being so close to his home in Centreville, figured it was for the Mrs.

This time.

Smooth devil.

Hair was still stringy, but haircut was recent. Jacket was on his arm with white dress shirt's sleeves rolled up as he shopped. Was missing the distinct walk he exhibited back at Midway. No combat injury like I'd thought. He was just a performer like me.

Next stop was wine where he chatted up a fine sister with twists about a nice, full-bodied red while I enjoyed a free sample of pinot noir nearby courtesy of one of the store's team members.

As he found his way to the pasta section, imagined he planned a romantic meal, along with the flowers, to make up for something he'd done. Maybe for the long hours he was putting in at Langley. Or maybe long schlong he was putting in someone else.

I gave up wasting thoughts on his life. Because even though he didn't know it yet, as of this morning, it had suddenly changed.

I approached him from one end of the aisle once we were alone. Just as he was filling a clear plastic container with rigatoni. While he bent over, fumbling with the release on the pasta, I spoke.

"You got it there, buddy?" I asked cordial enough in a faux Midwestern voice meant to disarm.

"Yeah," he spouted, focused on the task at hand. "My wife likes the shit at this store, so I'm making concessions. I'm more a steak 'n' potatoes kinda guy."

"I hear ya," I commented with a jocular chuckle. "Tell me, do you know if this entire section is gluten free?"

"You've got me there, pal," he said, satisfied with a full container as he finally turned to engage me. No armed security this time. And no me being at a disadvantage.

As his smiled morphed into a sour pucker, his eyes said it all.

"Hello, Nathan," I offered. My smile was still there.

"You," he hissed, his voice cracking unintentionally. "How . . . how?"

"Sometimes when you yank on a tiger's tail, you get bit," I said to Nathan Piatkowski of Tannerhouse Way in Centreville. Just before I smashed him in the face with a palm thrust followed by a spinning backfist that connected just behind his ear. Left the no longer mysterious Mr. Smith sprawled on the floor of the whole grains aisle in a creation of red wine and rigatoni al dente.

I exited the store at a brisk clip before anyone could call the cops on me. Back in my car, I drove around the side of Dick's Sporting Goods and parked once again. Opened a secure line on my phone where I sent an attachment to my *ghost in the machine* at 4Shizzle then messaged her.

Promised u a story, I typed.

This ain't my usual. But damn . . .

Just need u 2 wait b4 u post.

When?

Soon. Will get back 2 u.

I left Virginia, pleased with results so far. Drove into DC where I decided to dine at Georgia Brown's, having run on fumes since yesterday. Sat outside along Fifteenth Street Northwest waiting on my jerked catfish under the lights as the sun had retreated somewhere far west of the city.

Enough time had elapsed to call him on the cell phone I'd left inside his townhome. A townhome that was missing his wife, Sara, a school teacher at Ormond Stone Middle School, and their young son, Slade.

Wondered how many times he'd broken down crying since rushing home from Whole Foods and finding them missing. Wanted that despair to fester.

"Hello!" he yelled desperately as he answered on the second ring.

"Nathan, do I have your attention?" I calmly asked.

And here came my jerked catfish meal.

34

Arrived at the Port of Baltimore. Shipping vessels stacked with cargo and containers reminding me of season two of *The Wire*. I drove along looking for a particular warehouse, a good sign that they all started looking the same after awhile. Would make it a little harder for the former Mr. Smith if he grew a pair, came clean with his employer and decided to use his resources to find his family. But he wasn't going to do that. Not just yet.

Took it as a compliment that he feared me and what I might be capable of.

Still, I had other things with which to attend.

Like Sophia.

"Truth, what the fuck are you up to?" she asked.

"Kinda in the middle of something. Can we talk later?" I pushed back, knowing what the call was about.

"Look, I'm getting tired of you brushing me off. Ivan's dead, Truth."

"What are you talking about?" I asked straight-faced as I drove up to the warehouse I was looking for.

"He's dead. In New Orleans. Fuckin' dead," she groaned.

"What was he doing there? It's not Mardi Gras . . . or Southern Decadence," I dryly joked.

"You tell me. I know you had something to do with it, you bastard!" Sophia screamed. Wincing, I pulled my Bluetooth away from my ear.

"Now you're sounding paranoid. I'm not even in New Orleans. And I'm busy trying to stay alive, I can promise you that. Look . . . let me finish this then you'll have my undivided attention. See if we can figure this out," I offered.

"You promise?"

"Yes. Now I'll talk to you later. Be strong. Ivan would want that," I said, hearing those gunshots on the Algiers Ferry again. Most of NOPD's investigation would hit a dead end with them left to surmise Ivan was paid by Braxton Lewis's people.

I got out the car and knocked on the office door. Kept to the side in case somebody felt like shooting. Didn't know them like that to fully trust, but I was pressed for time when I called it in.

"*Que es?*" the voice barked in Spanish from behind the thick metal door.

"I brought lunch. Nathan's," I replied, the irony of the name being the same as Mr. Smith's real moniker unintentional.

The door came unlocked amid a shriek of metal on metal. A man in a black leather coat with a mask resting atop his head smiled, taking the bag of hot dogs and fries from me as he looked to make sure I was alone.

"Any problems?" I asked as I warily entered.

"Nah. They in there," he replied as he locked and bolted the door behind me, cocking his head in the direction of another room.

Four men with the distinct clown masks pulled over their faces saw me, talking among themselves before three left the other with their guests and came over. Clear of being identified, they removed their masks.

"Thank you," I said to them as they all took turns welcoming me to their little slice of heaven on the dock. Then hurried over to the hot dogs 'n' stuff.

"Oh," the second one, who looked to be Dominican, grunted as he remembered something. "This is for you," he said as he planted the digital recorder in my hand.

I pressed play, listening for a voice. "Perfect," I uttered, satisfied with what I heard. "Did you let that stuff slip out like I asked?"

"Yeah, yeah. And she was listenin' too," he volunteered. "Are you really the dude that found that fuckin' child molester for Arturo?" he asked, referring to his boss Arturo Diaz, the welterweight champion of the world.

"Nah. I just work for him. Like y'all do for Diaz," I lied.

"Man. You stupid," one of the other men chided him. "You know he ain't gonna be here for this."

"Can I borrow one of those?" I asked, referring to their clown masks. With a shrug, one was tossed into my hands as they continued to gorge on the hotdogs. Arturo's boy who was still on guard threw a mock salute at his fellow clown as I walked over. In a chair positioned in the corner was Sara Piatkowski, bound and blindfolded. Had her son Slade locked in another room with a Nintendo Wii and no restraints. I'd lured them from their house yesterday, claiming I worked with Nathan in town and that he'd been in a bad accident. Kept the neighbors disarmed too rather than having a van full of goons roll up and remove them forcibly. Let that part come later when we were down the road.

"How much longer?" my fellow clown asked, his voice muffled, but still revealing a heavy New York accent.

"Soon," I calmly replied.

I wandered off deeper into the warehouse, ready to indeed end it. While out of view, I removed the mask and placed a call to someone anxious to hear from me.

"Nathan, how'd you sleep?" I taunted upon his answering.

"Fuck you, nigger," he spat. I doubted his racist tendencies surfaced while he was impregnating Bricks's stripper sister down in NOLA. But I kept that knowledge to myself.

Rather than engage in name calling, I placed the digital recorder to the phone.

"Please. Please. I don't want to die!" his wife's recorded voice screamed. Pitch perfect before I ended the recording with a click.

"So . . . what's it going to be?" I asked Mr. Piatkowski, the man who just listened to his wife's pleas in stunning digital clarity.

"Now look here . . ."

"Don't stall. You'll only make it worse for her. And your kid."

"I'll kill you! I swear to God, I will—"

"Do what I say. You will do what I say," I uttered, completing his statement for him.

I checked my watch while he came to grips with his new reality. Just in case he was trying to track me through cell towers like I'd done back in the Pacific Northwest.

"Okay. Okay. How can I trust you?" he asked.

"You can't," I said calmly. "No one can trust me. But I did tell you that I don't work for free. I did my part in New Orleans, now I want to be compensated."

"I haven't received confirmation the DA's dead. Only that there was a shooting."

"Spin," I said succinctly. "I assure you Rodney Roy won't be magically gracing any cameras in our lifetime. Now about my compensation." What I was doing with Nathan's family would keep him off his game. Less concerned with his reasons for hiring me and my results. Instead, more focused on just getting through this with his wife and child safely home.

"How do I know you won't kill them if I do this?" he asked. Legit question.

"Because I didn't take you out yesterday when I could've. And because I'm only asking for one hundred grand. Something I know you can quickly pull together from whatever accounts you fund your little covert war games around the world. Small price to pay for keeping your job . . . and getting your family back unharmed. Then we never hear from one another again."

Silence.

"Tick tock, Mr. Piatkowski," I mocked. Felt marvelous turning that back on him.

"You win," he said. "I'll get your money."

"Excellent. Know that was hard for you to say. You'll receive your instructions for my money shortly. Don't fuck it up."

I hung up, removing the battery and SIM card. Lowered my borrowed mask once again as I returned to where Mrs. Piatkowski was being held. Needed to see her up close. Stood there for a minute before the blindfolded school teacher possessed of curly brown hair and slight frame. Let her sense my presence yet not know what I was about to do. Yanked her blindfold off, watching her flinch and blink at the sudden intrusion of light into her eyes. And as things came into focus, let the scary clown mask fill her entire field of vision.

Didn't say anything at first. Just kept canting my head as I let the creepiness set in, my shallow breathing my only sound.

Spitting at me, she finally shrieked, "You monster! What . . . what do you want?"

"Your husband knows what we want, Mrs. Piatkowski. But . . . for some reason, it seems he doesn't really care about your well-being," I began to spin from beneath my clown mask. With what she conveniently *overheard* earlier and now this . . .

This was going to be sweet.

So sweet.

35

Nathan Piatkowski arrived at Cleveland Hopkins International Airport. Flew in on Continental and, per my instructions that were waiting on him, took the taxi cab for the nine-mile trek downtown to the Ritz-Carlton Cleveland.

I'd avoided being anywhere near the airport. Remembered how much control he had back at Midway in Chicago, so instead guided him further and further beyond his comfort zone. When I got word that he'd arrived in the lobby of the Ritz, I sent a text on my phone to my friend at 4Shizzle.

OK to run it, I texted, referring to the story I'd sent to her previously.

Followed that up with a quick call to Arturo Diaz's boys back at the warehouse in BMore.

"One hour," I uttered, giving them instructions on when to release Piatkowski's family.

Then the disposable phone in my pocket rang.

"All right. I'm at the Ritz," he said, seeming weary and irritated. "And my wife and son better be here."

"I can assure you that both Sara and Slade are here and they miss you," I prodded. "But they're not at the Ritz."

"What the fuck!" he screamed.

"Change in plans. Walk over to the Renaissance Hotel. There will be a note left for you under the name of

Robert James at the front desk," I instructed. "And you better have my money," I added to keep him misled about my intent. He was going to pay all right. Just not in the manner he expected.

After hanging up, I broke that phone and discarded it in the hotel lobby garbage can I'd just opened. Fifteen minutes later, the former Mr. Smith strolled in from off the street. He stopped less than four feet from me as I remained in my guise as a janitor—a pillow in my shirt simulating a gut and some makeup on my face for effect—going about changing out the remaining garbage cans. With the Cleveland Indians having a home game, foot traffic was heavy in the lobby. Had gathered two full trash bags in my hands as I watched him retrieve his note then follow its instructions.

I shuffled over to the restroom, abandoning my trash bags by the door as I entered. Walked over to the two stalls marked as out of order. One was already occupied by him, so I entered the adjacent one. Quickly removed the pillow from my shirt and peeled away the makeup on my face.

"Here," I said, sliding a duffle bag under the divider. Had him switch out his clothes and into the set I'd provided. He held on to the money though, refusing to relinquish it without seeing his family first.

The two of us exited the lobby restroom, both wearing different clothing en route to the hotel elevator.

"You want to kill me," I stated as I pushed the button to take us to the eleventh floor. Kept my back to him while I whistled a tune, letting him know how little I took him as a threat.

"Yep. Knew you were smart when I recruited you," he snarkily commented.

"Recruit," I repeated. "That's what you call it? Felt more like a mandatory draft."

"Just a job I needed done."

"But why?" I asked, knowing he wouldn't respond. "No matter," I continued. "The DA's not dead anyway."

"What?" he blurted out, almost choking over my revelation.

"Oh. This is our floor. Let's go get your family," I stated, ignoring his shock and anger. Just another thing to give him a taste of the helplessness I'd felt at his hand.

At room 1106, I inserted the key and motioned for my guest to follow. He surveyed both ends of the hallway first, looking for anything amiss. When he was done, I motioned again then entered first. Entering the suite behind me and realizing it was empty, Piatkowski swung his money-filled duffle bag at my head. Frustration and anxiety taking their toll.

"Where are they?" he demanded as I blocked then ducked the hefty one hundred grand. A table lamp tumbled to the carpet from one of the swings.

"Calm down. Money first," I said as I wrapped him in a bear hug to restrain him. "And not if you're going to continue acting like a madman."

When he ceased fighting, I released him. But not without him giving me a final shove on the break. "I don't let go of this until I see them," he chided.

"Fine," I said as I strode to the connecting door of the adjacent suite. Unlocked it then opened to reveal what was just next door.

"Sara," he gasped, dropping his duffle bag at the sight of his wife bound in a chair before the window with a hood over her head.

"Nathan?" she called out from beneath the hood.

"Yes, honey! It's me!" he gushed, a genuine smile forming as he took a single cautious step into the suite. Looked like he wanted to cry. Then his distrustful nature kicked in as he looked for booby traps or some kind of setup. "Wait. Where's my boy? Where's Slade?" he asked, not taking a step farther.

"Here's the deal. Your son's in a different room in this hotel. You get your wife first," I said as I motioned for him to hand over the bag. "She'll tell you what room he's in."

"Nah. I'm holding on to the money until I make sure Sara's okay. Then you can take your fuckin' cash," he said as he snatched up his duffle again and backed toward his wife.

"Suit yourself," I relented. "But don't think you're leaving this room without giving me my money."

Piatkowski glared at me. Reaching into his bag, he pulled out a gun. The old double cross I'd been expecting. Looked to be a Sig Sauer P250.

"Think about your son, Nathan," I reminded him as he took aim. "This can still go down without any complications."

"Nathan?" the bound woman called out again as if on cue.

Piatkowski bit his lip and closed his eyes for a second as he refocused. Nodding at me, he lowered his gun slightly and continued to ease in her direction in front of the window. I stood immobile in the connecting doorway, my eyes cutting to the time on the clock.

He cautiously checked around his wife for any sort of wires or explosives before slowly raising the hood from off her head.

But things with me are rarely what they seem.

"A dummy," he mumbled, eyes staring in disbelief.

From behind my back, I pushed the tiny remote again.

"Nathan?" the speaker stowed inside the dummy called out again, mocking him.

A recording.

"Where is she?" he screamed, a little too loud for my comfort as he dropped the duffle bag and brought the gun sight back on me, taking steady aim with both hands.

The other connecting door along the opposite wall clicked at that moment, Piatkowski torn between two potential targets now. From the other suite entered five well-dressed and rather large armed men. The third one to fill the doorframe I knew well, having scrapped with the tree trunk a year ago in a South Beach pool.

But I'd seen him more recently than that.

Mere days ago.

During my layover at the Fort Lauderdale Airport when I was en route from New Orleans to BWI.

When I proposed burying the hatchet and making amends.

Amends with the tall, robed figure who just entered the suite.

Prince Abdel Al-Bin Sada.

A hush fell over the room as the towering yet wiry Arab stood at command behind a wall of Hugo Boss and Armani-covered bulk. I stood my ground and nodded at him.

He demanded that he be here for this perceived reckoning.

Piatkowski stared in disbelief at what was unfolding courtesy of me.

"Is this the one?" Prince Al-Bin Sada asked me of Piatkowski.

"Yes. Yes, Your Highness," I replied, faking humility as I averted my eyes. "He is my boss. Was my boss."

"Huh? *What the fuck are you talking about?*" Piatkowski snarled at me, out of sorts. "And what does the prince have to do with this?"

"As I said, he employed me for the job, Your Highness. Then wouldn't pay me. Most untrustworthy," I offered.

"Wait! This is all about not paying you for the job? *All this?*" he said, waving his handgun indiscriminately at the gathered throng. No one flinched, which seemed to spook Piatkowski even more.

"Sounds like he just admitted hiring this man, Your Highness," the HMIC—Head Monster in Charge—matter-of-factly offered to his boss. Most words I'd ever heard the man say.

The prince nodded, eyes flaring with hatred. "But where is my information?" he asked me while not taking his eyes off the man I'd just set up.

"It's on him, Your Highness. The flash drive's in his pocket," I calmly pointed out.

Before Piatkowski could dispute what I was saying, two of the prince's bodyguards rushed him. They were faster than their size would indicate, as I'd learned before. They drove both him and the faux Sara to the floor with a brutal, jarring thud, crushing his hand even as he still held on to his gun.

"Ow!" he yelped as several fingers snapped.

He was too overmatched beneath the seven-hundred-plus pounds of muscle to put up a fight as they pried the Sig Sauer from his swollen hand then removed a tiny flash drive from his pocket. A flash drive

I'd deposited moments ago when I bear hugged him. And on that flash drive it held all that Sophia had *borrowed* from the prince, including passwords to access his diverted funds.

Piatkowski had done enough double crosses and dirty jobs in his life. Had to realize he'd been royally played so to speak. Straining to speak, he looked at me. "My . . . my wi—" he tried to say.

"Is safe back home. Both she and your son. Unharmed," I assured him.

Wasn't totally evil.

He nodded, bowing down to his master with a faint smile that spoke of resignation.

"Are we done here, Your Highness?" I asked, daring to be insolent.

"Are there any copies?" Prince Al-Bin Sada inquired.

"No, Your Highness," I answered.

Rather than addressing me further, HMIC took charge. "You can go," he grunted as the prince left the suite with the flash drive secure in his hand. Was leaving his bodyguards behind to *disappear* Piatkowski, the man who, according to me, was the one behind Sophia's stealing of the prince's info. At our hasty meeting in the Fort Lauderdale Airport, I'd poured it on. Wove a tale of Piatkowski having coerced his favorite girl Aswad into betraying His Highness. The prince wanted to believe that someone had forced poor little Aswad into betraying him anyway. I just gave him a villain. Claimed the only way I could've gotten inside his compound in Miami was with the aid of someone like Piatkowski. Again, something he needed to hear . . . and believe.

"And the money?" I asked, pointing at the duffel bag.

"Take it," the prince said himself with a dismissive wave from the other room.

His imposing bodyguards paused their subduing of Piatkowski, graciously moving aside to allow me to snag the duffle bag. I squatted next to him as he attempted to get a hand on me; one final exercise in futility.

"This was never about the money," I said low enough to be heard by his ears only as I snatched the bag. "Good-bye, Mr. Smith."

Knowing he wasn't long for this world, Piatkowski didn't bother with any parting words as I left him to the prince's not-so-kindly graces.

I knew not to trust him. Even if I'd killed the DA for him, he would always be a threat to Collette . . . and to me.

But no more.

To his employers back in Langley, it would look like he suddenly up and ran off with a hundred grand of their money. Then once they got his wife to talk, she'd fill them in on what she overheard—a one-sided conversation where the men holding her appeared to argue with her husband over money he owed them. And where he told them to fuck off as he was skipping the country with his mistress.

Arturo Diaz's boys knew to drop the word "Barbados" before leaving Sara and Slade Piatkowski alone and unharmed in the warehouse. As good a lead as any for the U.S. government to begin looking for Nathan and their money.

Another quick change of clothes, which included a pair of new running shoes, and I left the Renaissance Hotel via the connected Tower City Center wearing Cleveland Indians fan gear. Once inside the mall, I blended into the crowd of rowdy baseball fans en route to the indoor walkway that would take us to Progressive Field for the big game.

And then I was gone.

Merrily shouting, "Let's go, Tribe!"

36

I left the ballpark, catching a cab to Cleveland Hopkins International Airport. When I got there, I planned on renting a car for the last leg of my trip. Pittsburgh was where I intended on stowing the money then flying out. In case the money was marked or something, I wasn't crazy enough to risk going through airport screening with it.

As my cab pulled up to the drop-off point for departures, I told the driver I'd get my duffle bag out myself. Paid him fifty dollars for getting me here so quick. He thanked me for my generosity after confirming it wasn't funny money.

"Ain't you missin' the game?" the mustached cabbie asked, acknowledging my baseball cap in his rearview mirror.

"Flight to catch. This trip was planned a long time ago and I ain't payin' no extra fees. Besides, did you see how they blew the lead last game? Believe me, I ain't gettin' my hopes up," I joked, having learned about the Indians' collapse only an hour ago.

"Yeah. You right. And I had money on dat game," he said with a hearty laugh. As I fetched my bag from the trunk then waved bye, I looked for any signs of having been followed. Back downtown, I'd zigged and zagged enough to throw off even the most seasoned professional. All seemed fine now.

Rather than entering the airport, I made my way to the rental car pickup point. Boarded the bus with the other customers then told the driver the name under which I'd made the reservation. While seated, I did a quick check to ensure my ID matched.

Received a call from Sophia just then. Probably wanting to make sure I was okay after pleading with her to share with me what she'd stolen from the prince.

And thank God she did.

"Hey," I said, answering as the bus prepared to pull away from the curb. For our listening pleasure, the driver hit the automated instructions which everyone proceeded to ignore.

"Is . . . is everything going to be okay now?" she asked. Sounded throaty. Congested. Like she'd been crying. Or doing something else that involved her nose.

"Yeah. We're good. Prince was appreciative to get his shit back," I mumbled into the phone. People were in their own little worlds, probably focused on their trips to the Rock and Roll Hall of Fame or just coming home, but I still kept my voice low.

A hand swatted at the side of the bus, startling everyone. Thought we'd run over something, but was just another customer too impatient to wait for the next bus. Big white dude with Oakley shades and a black golf shirt. From behind the mirrored orange lenses, he offered a quick apology to the rest of us then took a seat. When the driver asked him if he belonged to the ultra secret special privileges club, he said, "No." It would be the front desk for him, to wait in a long line, when we arrived at the rental place.

"And are you appreciative, Truth?" Sophia asked pointedly.

"Huh?" I muttered, my focus back on the conversation. "Of course."

"Then how come you don't love me?" she pushed, coming outta nowhere with that.

"Uh . . . can we talk later?"

"No! I'm tired of you putting me off unless you want something!" she yelled. Then just as quick, she dropped to a barely audible murmur. "No one's ever loved me. Not my parents. Not you. Not even Ivan. Because if he did, he wouldn't have left me," she said, no longer restraining her sobs.

Now she had my full attention.

Depression and anxiety plus drugs were a dangerous mix.

We arrived at the rental agency. The driver instructed those of us who already had reservations to exit and look for our names on the board. I took my cue and exited along with five other folks, cradling the duffle bag full of money against my side as I continued my conversation with Sophia.

"Do you need me to go out there? I can be there late tonight. Seriously."

"Naw, naw!" she ranted. "Just keep on playing your little games with people's lives. With all your lies 'n' shit. Because there will be one less person for you to fuck with."

Her desperation pumped a sense of urgency into me. Made me go even faster toward my numbered slot. Was a row of SUVs. "Sophia, listen to me. Don't talk like this," I urged. "This ain't you. You're stronger than this."

"Yeah. I'm stronger than a mofo, bitch," she cursed. "Strong enough to decide when I wanna go."

"And this ain't the time," I vowed as I slowed next to the Ford Explorer that was mine. "Hey . . . remember what good times we had in London?" I asked, trying to evoke better times for Sophia as I opened the passenger door and tossed the duffle bag inside.

"Yeah. I'll always remember them, baby. Always."

"Sophia!" I yelled as she hung up. I prepared to redial her.

And at that very moment, caught a glint of metal in the Explorer's window reflection.

I let the phone go, dropping flat to the pavement as whatever it was struck the bill of my baseball cap. As I rolled onto my back, the man's momentum carried him forward, stumbling over me and banging into the SUV's mirror. He couldn't brace himself because his hands were entangled in something.

The shiny object strung between his hands, which I'd seen, was the exposed wire of a garrote.

If he'd gotten it over my head and around my neck, I would've been dead. No doubt about it.

No time to dwell on it, I kicked as hard as I could at the back of the man's leg. When his leg buckled, I struck him with another kick, this time targeting his kidneys. As he grimaced from the pain, the garrote slipped from his grasp. Then he rolled from any further kicks of mine, gathering himself to get back to his feet. As he turned to come at me again, I got a look at his face.

Sunglasses and all.

Was the man in the Oakley shades from the airport bus.

But was also the unmarked security agent from Midway Airport. The one when I first met Mr. Smith. If he was helping Piatkowski then, he was probably the only one Piatkowski trusted with his secrets.

I'd gotten too cocky. Sloppy even. Knew Piatkowski came alone, but didn't consider he'd have someone trailing behind. Probably came in on the next flight and had been tracking me through something in the duffle bag since I left the hotel.

As I crawled backward, my shoes digging in for traction, sunglasses grinned at me just as he did that day at Midway. He was intent on me not leaving this parking lot alive.

And he was a loose end for me.

"It's over. You won't be seeing your friend again. Feel like being reasonable?" I asked without moving. Maybe sharing some of the proceeds inside the SUV would suffice in reining in this trained attack dog.

His answer was to pull a short carbon fiber knife from his belt. Definite military background by his moves. As he took a cautious step forward, he stepped on my phone. Reminded me what I was doing when he attacked me.

And what I needed to do now.

I did a quick roll backward to get to my feet. Made him think I was going to make a run for it. Let him rush me with a knife thrust that caught me dead in the center of my gut, its ferocity lifting me off the ground. Prepared for his kill strike, I held on to his wrist for dear life, limiting how far he could drive the blade into my body. When he tried to retract the blade and thrust again, I still held on. His surprise over my still being among the living was brief, but allowed me all I needed. I launched toward him, landing a head butt dead in the center of his face. Took joy in the contact as I heard his nose crack. As he wobbled and loosened his grip on the blade, I released his wrist. Before he could pull his blade from out of my stomach, I cupped my hands, bringing them to bear across both his ears with a simultaneous pop. He howled from the double shock to his nervous system, bringing his hands up to weakly defend himself.

His blade fell to the ground, but absent any blood.

Knowing he planned on ending it as quickly as me, I kicked him in the nuts like I was going for a field goal. No glamour in fighting except in the movies. As he fell to one knee, I grasped the luggage rack on the Explorer and used it to vault over him. He swung wild, catching me with a lucky strike, but my momentum carried me. With one hop, I snatched up the garrote he'd tried to use on me and dove onto his back. Where he failed, I was successful in whipping the wire over his head, cinching it against his throat, pulling, then twisting. He reached back, trying to gouge my eyes, but I turned my face away and held on.

His adrenaline rocketed, knowing what it meant just as I did. We rolled along on the ground beside the Explorer, his feet kicking wildly as the struggle became more and more desperate. Fingers trying to find any slack as he gasped for air. But between the blood seeping down his throat from the broken nose and the tightening of the garrote, he found none. Seeing the feet of other rental customers coming down the aisle, I pulled him closer and wrapped my legs around him for control. Inched both of us beneath the SUV and as out of view as we could get as the fight left his body. He was much stronger than me and had the element of surprise at first. But it made him lazy, only taking one mistake to cost you everything.

Wondered if that thought went through his mind as his life ebbed then faded.

I counted the minutes down after his struggles ended, trying to regain some calm before fully releasing the garrote. The wire had dug into his throat, exposing raw flesh which I checked for signs of a pulse. I flexed my sore fingers as I dared to move away, muscles twitching and spent as I came down off my adrenaline rush.

Needed to get out from under the Explorer now, but I reached over his body for my phone instead. It was still intact, so I tried Sophia again.

No answer.

I repeated the action several more times, but to no avail.

Didn't leave a message.

Instead, I hurriedly dialed the number to somebody in her area.

"It's me," I said when the person answered. Tried to sound calm and in control when I really wasn't.

"Ain't seen him around there in a minute," he reported, referring to Ivan. And being one of the people I paid to monitor Sophia and Ivan's bad habits.

"Look, I know that. Just listen. I need you to go by the apartment and check on her."

"You mean like knock on the door?" he asked while I pulled the Oakley sunglasses under the Explorer. "'Cause I like to just stay back, y'know. Watch and report. Like we agreed."

"Well I need you to knock on the door this time. Hell, kick the door open if you have to. I think she's done something stupid."

"Aww, man. Sorry to hear that. But listen . . . I can't make it around there today," he said. "Kid's birthday party. And everybody over."

"Listen. I don't care if it's you or just someone you trust, but somebody needs to go there. Now," I growled as I arose, wiping off the dust from my clothes and removing a pillow, which I'd used to alter my appearance and absorb the blade, from under my shirt. I opened the passenger door again, prepared to search through the duffle bag for whatever was used to track me here. I continued, "'Cause if something happens to her, then something's going to happen to you. Am I clear?"

"Yeah, yeah. I gotcha. Roger that," he replied nervously.

Fifteen minutes later, a man by the name of Andre Hollins from Milwaukee, Wisconsin, departed the rental car lot in a Ford Explorer, destined for Pittsburgh with his Oakley-wearing passenger *asleep* in the seat next to him.

But only the driver would arrive at the end of the trip.

Along the way, I still tried to reach Sophia.

But she never answered.

37

One Month Later
El Paso, TX

Things in New Orleans didn't quite have that fairy tale ending. Sure Rodney Roy was alive, but he was removed from the Bricks Lewis case by the governor. In a letter circulated to the press by the Republican governor up in Baton Rouge, and in a possible political move to discredit the traditional New Orleans Democrat Roy, he cited Rodney's removal from the high profile case due to *the potential unseemly appearance of him trying a case while having a personal vendetta against the defendant for an attack on him for which no credible connection has been established.*

The assistant DAs did what I thought they would and botched the case on a technicality, resulting in Bricks Lewis being released back on to the street until they decided whether to retry the case. I was sure, by that time, the sparse witnesses would be even less willing to cooperate. Bricks celebrated his freedom by throwing a major party, complete with appearances by some of the city's major rappers, in the New Orleans Arena just down the street from City Hall.

The whole thing damaged Rodney's political career, but worse than that was the implied threat by Bricks on his family . . . and my daughter.

I'd protect her . . . and Summer even if they didn't want me to.

Even from afar.

I sat casually at a square table bordered by four cushioned chairs. Wore army camouflage BDUs adorned with the insignia of a lieutenant with the First Armored Division from over at Fort Bliss. An older gentleman in golf shoes had just come over and shaken my hand, thanking me for my service. Said he'd served also and wanted to talk too long about where I'd been stationed, but I endured.

I was at the Lone Star Golf Club on Hawkins Boulevard, reading the lunch menu at the Sandtrap restaurant. Waiter recommended the beef tacos, considered the best in town. So I decided to go with that and a Diet Coke, but told him I awaited a lunch guest. Had a delicate business meeting arranged here. Wasn't sure if they were going to show, but for now I would be content to just be heard.

A middle-aged Hispanic gentleman with a coif of full black hair entered fresh off the course. Mostly everyone in here knew him, which he acknowledged, cracking jokes and trading waves with all who were interested. The gregarious man was accompanied by two young boys who looked to be around twelve or thirteen. About the same age as my Sasha. When he approached my table, I stood up to greet him and his young wards.

"Please, please, sit, my friend," Jorge "George" Pinero, businessman and city council member, urged with a congenial smile and a hearty pat on the back.

"Thank you, sir," I said as he motioned for three teas for him and the young men. George sat across the square table from me, with a friend on each side. "Links been good to you today?" I asked.

"Yes, yes. Teaching my two friends here some of the finer skills that will do them well in business one day," he replied. I looked into the eyes of the two young men who remained unidentified. They showed neither the intimidation nor fascination for the adult world to which George referred. *I'll be damned.* They were his security force. Battle-hardened young soldiers in the drug war raging down in Juarez just across the border. Shouldn't have been too surprised as that's why I was here.

"Thank you for seeing me," I said. "I know you're a very busy person in the community and appreciate your fitting me into your schedule."

"When my constituents received word, I had to come. You are either very serious or very foolish, my friend. Are you even in the military?" he probed, eliciting a grin from one of the boys. Probably had more experience with firearms than I ever would.

I ignored his question, simply smiling back. "Your associate in New Orleans . . . Braxton Lewis," I began.

"I don't have associates in New Orleans," George stopped me. "Most of my stuff is local with a little bit around the rest of west Texas and some imports from Juarez. I do hear they have a nice Mardi Gras out there though."

"I understand. Just wanted to inform you about this Braxton Lewis. In case your constituents' business interests ever intersect with his."

"Proceed," he said.

"Bricks, as he's known on the streets of New Orleans and in the flashy rap lyrics that mention him, works for the gringos."

"Which gringos?" he asked, his interest piqued.

"This country's government. He tells them secrets; gives them intel on your constituents."

"Are you calling this Bricks person a—*how do they say it in the flashy rap lyrics?*—a 'snitch'?"

"*Sí.*"

"And why should we believe you? Someone who neither I . . . nor my constituents have ever met?" he asked.

I slowly retrieved my iPad, then proceeded to pull up a popular gossip Web site. 4Shizzle, if you must know. Slid it across the table for him to view. "See. Common knowledge," I remarked. 4Shizzle's article was titled: RAPPERS: FROM WE LOVE BRICKS TO DON'T BE A SNITCH? SAY IT AIN'T SO! The story went on about how Braxton Lewis has a close relationship with people deep within the U.S. government, hinting that they might be DEA. The 4Shizzle article had made its rounds by now. Other urban gossip sites piled on, creating a feeding frenzy on the Net. Had a lot in the hip hop community wondering if Bricks was indeed a snitch with connections inside the U.S. government. After Bricks's big release party, certain rappers had begun distancing themselves for fear of losing street cred. Some even denied being there despite the photos to the contrary.

Was interesting watching George Pinero: councilman eyeing the article as George Pinero: cartel representative. Him contemplating a compromised business partner while trying to hide his concern. Even our waiter knew better than to approach our table with our drinks during this conversation.

"You're slow with your intel if the gossip sites have already been reporting this," I chided. Maybe a little too aggressive for the young'uns as they both scowled at me.

"And what do you get out of this, Lieutenant Tucker?" he asked, mocking the name on my uniform.

"It's personal. I have some issues with Bricks's government friend. Brick's sister, the stripper, has a kid with this gringo. Talk about sleeping with the enemy. Word in Washington . . . and Langley," I added before continuing, "is that he ran off somewhere and is waiting to send for her when it's clear. Something happens to Bricks then maybe he surfaces."

"I see. Why do I think you're a company man," he said, referring to the CIA. "And looking for one of your own. Giving me this personal revenge bullshit while using us to flush him out."

"Can't confirm or deny. Just stating the facts. What you . . . or your constituents do about your business partner is just that . . . your business," I said, placing a twenty on the table to pay for drinks 'n' stuff. "Enjoy your afternoon of golf, Councilman. *Muchachos,*" I offered as I stowed my iPad then got up to leave. One of the kids made an aggressive move to stop me, but was restrained by the cooler headed adult in charge. George Pinero thinking I was really CIA would ensure I'd get out of El Paso alive. People thinking Piatkowski was still alive and on the run, instead of shark food for the prince's pets, was a good thing, too.

And knowing how serious the cartels took this sort of thing, Braxton Lewis would never pose a threat to the Roy family or my daughter again.

Can't say the city of New Orleans would miss him either.

38

Epilogue
Ninety days later

I stood beside Sophia at Inglewood Park Cemetery, holding her hand. Yesterday, she was released from rehab up in the Bay Area. My people had gotten to her in time when she attempted suicide and managed to get her checked in discreetly and an alias for me to set her on her journey back.

I was waiting for her when she got out, prepared for whatever she needed to dish out. Instead, she hugged me and thanked me for caring. She wanted to come here, so I drove her down I-5, the drive being therapeutic for both of us.

"Here," I said, handing her a duffle bag I'd been holding on to. One free of any tracking devices.

She unzipped it, briefly running her hand through the stacks. Then she zipped it back, tactically shaking it to determine its weight. "That info on the prince was worth a whole lot more," she groused after her impromptu analysis.

"Not if you're not around to enjoy it," I commented inappropriately at the moment considering where we were.

"True I guess," Sophia commented, not busting my chops. Maybe her convalescence had changed her. "But

I'm just glad I kept a copy," she revealed with a cackle. Typical Sophia rearing its head. "Thank you," she said as she gave me a gentle kiss on the cheek.

"You're welcome."

"Know what really happened to him?" she asked, looking at Ivan's gravesite. Someone had anonymously paid for it. A decent burial for a less-than-decent man.

"Yeah," I replied, reciting what I'd had three months for which to prepare. "Did some checking with my contacts down in New Orleans. Heard a few things. That Ivan owed protection money to some Russians while he was on lock. That shit down there was to pay off his debt."

"Damn," she spat with a shudder in her voice she tried to control. But failed to do so. "If he would've just told me, I . . . I could've . . ."

"Shhhh. Shhh," I hushed, holding her tight. "I guess he wanted to man-up for a change. Stop using women and take care of the debt himself. I guess he was trying to protect you from them. In a way, I guess he was a hero."

We stayed there for a while. I just held her, saying nothing else. Neither lie nor truth being acceptable, so silence protected us both.

When she was ready, she walked over to his headstone, placing her hand on it as she shared a private moment with Ivan. I left the two of them alone and walked back to the car.

I removed my jacket and sat on the hood of the Chevy Camaro, staring up at the afternoon sky from behind my black sunglasses. Thought back to my time in SoCal as that small child with the mother who dared to dream she could be something more.

Now I had a child.

Last month, Bricks Lewis was brutally murdered. Gunned down in parking lot of the strip club Fancy's; presumably by a rival who was the cartel's new business partner for the Gulf Coast. A rival who bore no animosity or ill will toward the Roy family.

"What are you daydreaming about?" Sophia asked, back from whatever closure she sought.

"Nothing," I replied matter-of-factly. "Ready to go?"

"Yeah. But I don't know where," she said, jokingly shaking the duffle bag once more. "I'm not going back to the apartment in Stockton. Place is toxic. Maybe I'll check into a nice five-star hotel. One with a spa."

"Tell you what," I said, hopping off the car's hood. "I got a place up in Seattle. Private. On the beach with lovely views. Clean air. You can stay there with me. Help you settle back in. Then whatever you do after that is on you. But I gotta warn you . . . my neighbor thinks I'm gay."

Sophia laughed; a good hearty one that brought color to her face. "Truth, are you letting me into your private world?" she asked.

"Hey. I don't have any family. Besides, we all we got," I chuckled, taking her by the hand as I opened the car door for her.

Thoughts of a dazzling little ballerina down in New Orleans that would one day grace the world stage filled me with pride. Pride that I had a hand in creating something flawless.

And so unlike me.

"Uh . . . Ain't it kinda cold up there?" Sophia bristled as I began to close her door.

"Not as cold as me," I joked, slamming it shut.

ORDER FORM
URBAN BOOKS, LLC
78 E. Industry Ct
Deer Park, NY 11729

Name: (please print): ______________________________

Address: ______________________________

City/State: ______________________________

Zip: ______________________________

QTY	TITLES	PRICE
	16 On The Block	$14.95
	A Girl From Flint	$14.95
	A Pimp's Life	$14.95
	Baltimore Chronicles	$14.95
	Baltimore Chronicles 2	$14.95
	Betrayal	$14.95
	Black Diamond	$14.95
	Black Diamond 2	$14.95
	Black Friday	$14.95
	Both Sides Of The Fence	$14.95
	Both Sides Of The Fence 2	$14.95
	California Connection	$14.95

Shipping and handling-add $3.50 for 1st book, then $1.75 for each additional book.
Please send a check payable to:

Urban Books, LLC

Please allow 4-6 weeks for delivery

ORDER FORM
URBAN BOOKS, LLC
78 E. Industry Ct
Deer Park, NY 11729

Name: (please print):___________________________________

Address: ___________________________________

City/State: ___________________________________

Zip: ___________________________________

QTY	TITLES	PRICE
	California Connection 2	$14.95
	Cheesecake And Teardrops	$14.95
	Congratulations	$14.95
	Crazy In Love	$14.95
	Cyber Case	$14.95
	Denim Diaries	$14.95
	Diary Of A Mad First Lady	$14.95
	Diary Of A Stalker	$14.95
	Diary Of A Street Diva	$14.95
	Diary Of A Young Girl	$14.95
	Dirty Money	$14.95
	Dirty To The Grave	$14.95

Shipping and handling-add $3.50 for 1st book, then $1.75 for each additional book.

Please send a check payable to:

Urban Books, LLC

Please allow 4-6 weeks for delivery

ORDER FORM
URBAN BOOKS, LLC
78 E. Industry Ct
Deer Park, NY 11729

Name: (please print):___________________________________

Address: ___________________________________

City/State: ___________________________________

Zip: ___________________________________

QTY	TITLES	PRICE
	Gunz And Roses	$14.95
	Happily Ever Now	$14.95
	Hell Has No Fury	$14.95
	Hush	$14.95
	If It Isn't love	$14.95
	Kiss Kiss Bang Bang	$14.95
	Last Breath	$14.95
	Little Black Girl Lost	$14.95
	Little Black Girl Lost 2	$14.95
	Little Black Girl Lost 3	$14.95
	Little Black Girl Lost 4	$14.95
	Little Black Girl Lost 5	$14.95

Shipping and handling-add $3.50 for 1st book, then $1.75 for each additional book.
Please send a check payable to:
Urban Books, LLC
Please allow 4-6 weeks for delivery